Imprisonment

Other Books of Related Interest:

GLOBALVIEWPOINTS

Imprisonment

Noah Berlatsky, Book Editor

GREENHAVEN PRESS
A part of Gale, Cengage Learning

GALE
CENGAGE Learning™

Detroit • New York • San Francisco • New Haven, Conn • Waterville, Maine • London

Christine Nasso, *Publisher*
Elizabeth Des Chenes, *Managing Editor*

© 2010 Greenhaven Press, a part of Gale, Cengage Learning

Gale and Greenhaven Press are registered trademarks used herein under license.

For more information, contact:
Greenhaven Press
27500 Drake Rd.
Farmington Hills, MI 48331-3535
Or you can visit our Internet site at gale.cengage.com

For product information and technology assistance, contact us at

Gale Customer Support, 1-800-877-4253
For permission to use material from this text or product, submit all requests online at www.cengage.com/permissions

Further permissions questions can be emailed to permissionrequest@cengage.com

Articles in Greenhaven Press anthologies are often edited for length to meet page requirements. In addition, original titles of these works are changed to clearly present the main thesis and to explicitly indicate the author's opinion. Every effort is made to ensure that Greenhaven Press accurately reflects the original intent of the authors. Every effort has been made to trace the owners of copyrighted material.

Cover image by John Moore/Getty Images.

LIBRARY OF CONGRESS CATALOGING-IN-PUBLICATION DATA

Imprisonment / Noah Berlatsky, book editor.
    p. cm. -- (Global viewpoints)
    Includes bibliographical references and index.
    ISBN 978-0-7377-4717-1 (hardcover) -- ISBN 978-0-7377-4718-8 (pbk.)
    1. Imprisonment--Juvenile literature. I. Berlatsky, Noah.
    HV8705.I47 2010
    365--dc22
                                                                2009045717

Printed in the United States of America
1 2 3 4 5 6 7 14 13 12 11 10

Contents

Chapter 1: The Purpose of Imprisonment

To understand why prison populations have been growing in Europe, it is important to understand why people
are imprisoned. In the West, the four main reasons given
for imprisoning criminals are punishment, deterrence,
reform, and protection of the public.

In recent years, New Zealanders have demanded harsher
sentences for criminals. The emphasis on retribution is
against Catholic teaching and produces a more violent
and fearful society. Instead, crime policy should focus on
cause, prevention, and rehabilitation.

Most Mexican people have traditionally held Catholic beliefs about redemption. A wave of drug-related violence
and civilian deaths, however, have led people to call for
harsher punishments including life imprisonment and
the death penalty.

Statistics show that through the 1990s the United States
increased rates of imprisonment and saw crime fall, while
England and Wales reduced rates of imprisonment and
saw crime rise. This suggests that the British government's
plan to promote alternatives to prison will actually increase crime rates.

Chapter 2: Sentencing and Imprisonment

Chapter 3: Prison Conditions

Chapter 4: Political Prisoners

Foreword

"The problems of all of humanity can only be solved by all of humanity."
—Swiss author Friedrich Dürrenmatt

Global interdependence has become an undeniable reality. Mass media and technology have increased worldwide access to information and created a society of global citizens. Understanding and navigating this global community is a challenge, requiring a high degree of information literacy and a new level of learning sophistication.

Building on the success of its flagship series, *Opposing Viewpoints*, Greenhaven Press has created the *Global Viewpoints* series to examine a broad range of current, often controversial topics of worldwide importance from a variety of international perspectives. Providing students and other readers with the information they need to explore global connections and think critically about worldwide implications, each *Global Viewpoints* volume offers a panoramic view of a topic of widespread significance.

Drugs, famine, immigration—a broad, international treatment is essential to do justice to social, environmental, health, and political issues such as these. Junior high, high school, and early college students, as well as general readers, can all use *Global Viewpoints* anthologies to discern the complexities relating to each issue. Readers will be able to examine unique national perspectives while, at the same time, appreciating the interconnectedness that global priorities bring to all nations and cultures.

Material in each volume is selected from a diverse range of sources, including journals, magazines, newspapers, nonfiction books, speeches, government documents, pamphlets, organization newsletters, and position papers. *Global Viewpoints* is truly global, with material drawn primarily from international sources available in English and secondarily from U.S. sources with extensive international coverage.

Features of each volume in the *Global Viewpoints* series include:

- An **annotated table of contents** that provides a brief summary of each essay in the volume, including the name of the country or area covered in the essay.

- An **introduction** specific to the volume topic.

- A **world map** to help readers locate the countries or areas covered in the essays.

- For each viewpoint, an **introduction** that contains notes about the author and source of the viewpoint explains why material from the specific country is being presented, summarizes the main points of the viewpoint, and offers three **guided reading questions** to aid in understanding and comprehension.

- **For further discussion** questions that promote critical thinking by asking the reader to compare and contrast aspects of the viewpoints or draw conclusions about perspectives and arguments.

- A worldwide list of **organizations to contact** for readers seeking additional information.

- A **periodical bibliography** for each chapter and a **bibliography of books** on the volume topic to aid in further research.

- A comprehensive **subject index** to offer access to people, places, events, and subjects cited in the text, with the countries covered in the viewpoints highlighted.

Global Viewpoints is designed for a broad spectrum of readers who want to learn more about current events, history, political science, government, international relations, economics, environmental science, world cultures, and sociology—students doing research for class assignments or debates, teachers and faculty seeking to supplement course materials, and others wanting to understand current issues better. By presenting how people in various countries perceive the root causes, current consequences, and proposed solutions to worldwide challenges, *Global Viewpoints* volumes offer readers opportunities to enhance their global awareness and their knowledge of cultures worldwide.

Introduction

> *"It would be nice to live in a society where there were no prisons, just as it would be nice if there were no hospitals because there was no illness. But until someone steps forward with a ten-year plan to Make Crime History, jails are here to stay."*
>
> —*Nick Herbert,*
> Guardian, *July 27, 2008.*

Prison is the standard punishment for serious crime. Most people in the United States and abroad accept this. Some activists, however, argue that prison is unjust and should be abolished. Julia Sudbury, in an article in the *Guardian* on July 26, 2008, declared, "Many of us believe that the prison, like the institution of slavery, will one day be viewed as an obsolete and shameful relic of history." Sudbury went on to hope for "a world without prisons."

Usually when advocates talk about alternatives to prison, they are referring to treatment, training, and supervision that are less invasive than incarceration. Darryl Fears, writing in the *Washington Post* on October 12, 2008, reported that U.S. officials were looking into "treatment programs for nonviolent drug users and employment training for minor parole violators." Fears noted that these programs were intended to reduce prison overcrowding, and were also thought by some experts to reduce recidivism (return to prison) rates. Sheri M. Whitley and Jeannie Yip in the July 13, 2006, *Columbia News* noted that alternatives to prison work about as well in reducing recidivism as prison does, and that they "cost significantly less than prison."

Fines are another, and perhaps the most popular, means of inflicting punishment without imprisonment. In "Fine Versus Imprisonment," a January 30, 2008, article on the Social Science Research Network Web site, Tarun Jain, an advocate at the Supreme Court of India, argues, "Fines are comparably effective to imprisonment and enrich rather than impoverish society. Accordingly, society should impose fines rather than imprisonment whenever feasible." Jain admits, however, that fines are often seen as allowing offenders to pay to commit crime, rather than as punishment. In addition, fines are seen as less damaging for the wealthy than for the poor. Jain concludes that fines are not politically acceptable for many crimes, even though prisons are very costly and often inhumane. David D. Friedman in "Rational Criminals and Profit-Maximizing Police: Gary Becker's Contribution to the Economic Analysis of Law and Law Enforcement," a chapter in *The New Economics of Human Behavior*, points out another problem with fines: Some people "are judgment proof—they do not have enough money to pay a fine high enough to represent an adequate punishment."

One alternative to prison that used to be very popular is corporal punishment. Corporal punishment is the deliberate infliction of pain upon a wrongdoer. Often, corporal punishment is meant to humiliate and inflict pain. Thus, whippings in ancient Rome were often performed in public. Similarly, the stocks device used in medieval Europe was designed to restrain criminals in public view. The offender was often kicked or struck by passersby. Other corporal punishments have included amputation, branding, blinding, and keelhauling. Keelhauling was a type of naval punishment in the seventeenth and eighteenth centuries that involved pulling an offender underwater from one side of the wooden ship to the other. Just as other kinds of corporal punishment, keelhauling could result in death.

In modern times, most Western nations have viewed corporal punishment of any sort as cruel and inhumane. Amnesty International "opposes the use of corporal punishment as a violation of the right not to be subjected to torture or cruel, inhuman or degrading treatment or punishment guaranteed by Article 5 of the Universal Declaration of Human Rights," as stated in a June 22, 2000, article. The same Amnesty International article makes it clear that corporal punishment is still used in some parts of the world. In Singapore, for example, those convicted of "attempted murder, armed robbery, immigration offenses, and vandalism" among other crimes may be subjected to caning, according to Pam Soltani in a 2003 *Pacific Rim Magazine* article. Other countries such as Saudi Arabia, Sudan, Botswana, and Tanzania also use judicial whippings as punishment.

A last alternative to imprisonment is the death penalty. Just as corporal punishment, the death penalty has been in use for thousands of years. And like corporal punishment, the use of the death penalty is now considered inhumane by most human rights organizations. The death penalty has been banned in many nations including all of Europe. Significant levels of public support for capital punishment continue, however, even in nations that have abolished the practice. For example, South Africa abolished the death penalty in 1997. After that, crime rates climbed and partially as a result, 72 percent of respondents in an Angus Reid poll published on May 14, 2006, wanted to reinstate the death penalty for certain crimes.

Many nations do retain the death penalty. Iran, Saudi Arabia, Pakistan, Iraq, and the United States all execute prisoners. According to the Death Penalty Information Center, the nation with the largest number of executions in 2008 was China, with 1,718 reported executions.

An important point to note about the options discussed here is that, for the most part, they tend to be used as additions to prison terms rather than as real alternatives to it. Criminals who are executed are usually first placed in prison; offenders who receive whippings generally also serve prison time. Similarly, a punishment may often include a fine and a prison term, and even drug treatment programs can exist alongside traditional prison regimes. James Q. Wilson, a proponent of imprisonment as a punishment for crime, told *Reason* in a February 1995 interview about a pending crime bill, "I like building more prisons. I like the drug courts." For Wilson, drug courts, which move offenders into treatment, can coexist with more prison construction; the first does not have to replace the second. When even alternatives to incarceration seem to rely on incarceration to some extent, Sudbury's "world without prisons" seems very distant.

Global Viewpoints: Imprisonment looks at some of the important issues surrounding imprisonment including the purposes of imprisonment, sentencing and prison, prison conditions, and political prisoners.

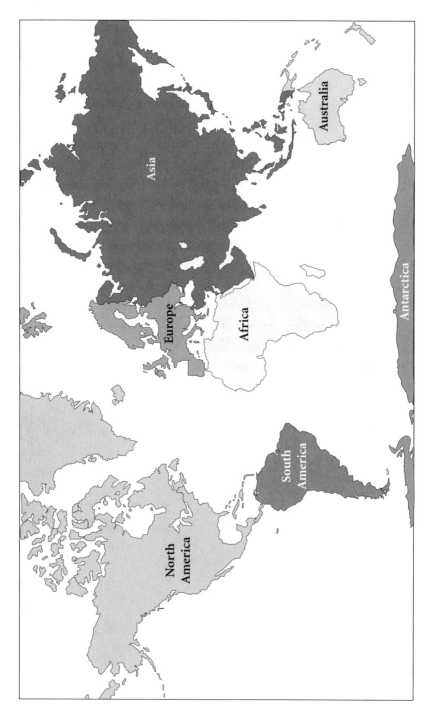

CHAPTER 1

The Purpose of Imprisonment

In Europe, There Are Four Main Justifications for Imprisonment

Council of Europe

The Council of Europe is an organization of forty-seven European member states working toward European integration. In the following viewpoint, the Council of Europe looks at the purposes of imprisonment to understand the growth of prison populations. The council states that the four main reasons for imprisoning criminals in the West are punishment, deterrence, reform, and protection of the public. The council argues that imprisonment is not very effective as a form of deterrence, reform, or protection. These rationales, and the belief that imprisonment should be used to punish even relatively minor crimes, have contributed to the growth of prison populations in Europe.

As you read, consider the following questions:

1. According to the viewpoint, what is the difference between individual deterrence and general deterrence?
2. What is the name of the argument that states that imprisonment can be used to lock away violent, persistent criminals and thus protect the public?
3. What form of imprisonment was used in the former Soviet Union?

Council of Europe, *European Prison Rules*, Strasbourg Cedex: Council of Europe Publishing, 2006, pp. 106–111. Copyright © Council of Europe, June 2006. Reproduced by permission.

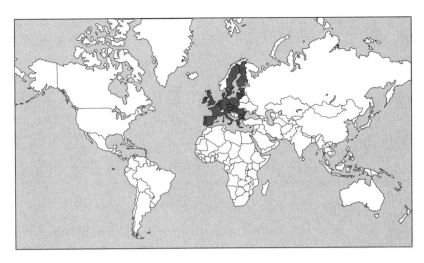

In trying to discover why rates of imprisonment in many countries have increased, even though there have not been comparable changes in rates or seriousness of crime, one should first consider what prison is meant to achieve and what society expects of it. This question of purpose is an important one because unless there is some clarity about this it will be difficult to discover whether or not imprisonment is effective. If we wish to know whether or not prison achieves its purposes we have to understand what these are. In the Western tradition there have generally been four main justifications for imprisoning a convicted offender. They are punishment, deterrence, reform and protection of the public. . . .

Imprisonment as Punishment

The essential feature of imprisonment in a democratic state is that it is a form of punishment or retribution imposed on an individual by a legitimate judicial authority in response to some legal wrong that the individual has committed. All member states of the Council of Europe [an organization of European states] have abolished the use of the death penalty and corporal punishment as judicial punishments. This leaves imprisonment as the most severe punishment available to any court. A central factor influencing levels of imprisonment in a country is the decision by a society about how much punishment it wishes to inflict on those who break the criminal law. Such a decision is likely to be based not solely on criminal justice considerations, such as rates of crime, but also on political and social factors. An understanding of this fact goes some way to explaining the discrepancy in rates of imprisonment between countries which do not appear to have any noticeable difference in crime rates.

Throughout the majority of the 20th century there was a consensus in most western European countries that the punishment of imprisonment should be reserved for those who had committed the most serious crimes and this remains the view of the Council of Europe. However, this principle is no longer universally accepted and the increase in rates of imprisonment in a number of countries can be traced to recent tendencies to imprison offenders who might previously have received non-prison sentences and also to impose longer sentences than was previously the case. In addition, there has been a growing tendency in some situations to make use of forms of preventive detention, for example, by means of sentences of indeterminate length.

Another important factor affecting the number of people in prison has been the decision in most countries to respond to the major social problem of drug abuse through criminal justice channels. There is general agreement that there should be severe punishment for major drug suppliers. It is not clear that taking a similarly punitive approach to those involved with illegal drugs for their own use or in petty drug dealing as a means of feeding their personal habit is an efficient method of tackling drug abuse as a social problem. This report is not a place to enter into this debate. However, it should be noted that one immediate consequence of this approach has been the incarceration of increasing numbers of drug abusers and of people who commit property crime in order to feed their drug habit. In general terms, punishing such people by sending them to prison does little to encourage them to break their habit and many of them are recidivist offenders.

"Despite lack of evidence about the efficacy of prison as a deterrent, politicians in a number of European jurisdictions have responded to concerns about crime by introducing more punitive criminal justice legislation."

Imprisonment as Deterrent

In terms of criminal justice, there are two main forms of deterrence: individual and general. Individual deterrence occurs when the prospect of being sent to prison deters an individual from committing a specific crime, or when the fact of having been sent to prison makes one decide never to commit crime again. General deterrence exists when we see someone else being sent to prison for an offence and that makes us decide that we had better not commit a similar offence for fear that the same might happen to us.

The high levels of repeat offending among those who have been served a prison sentence suggest that imprisonment does not act as an effective form of deterring individuals from crime, although we cannot calculate how many crimes are avoided because potential criminals are deterred by the prospect of imprisonment. The most important factor in terms of deterrence is certainty, or at least a high probability, of detection, rather than an anticipation of punishment.

Despite lack of evidence about the efficacy of prison as a deterrent, politicians in a number of European jurisdictions have responded to concerns about crime by introducing more punitive criminal justice legislation and by calling for more punitive sentences. These factors have contributed to increased prison populations.

Imprisonment for Rehabilitation

The concept of prison as a place of personal reform grew from the 19th century onwards in a number of western European countries. The notion that prison can be a place where individuals can be taught to change their behaviour is attractive on a number of counts. In the first place, it provides a positive justification for what would otherwise be a negative form of punishment of the criminal. The notion of prison as a place where personal reform can be engineered and encouraged is also attractive to the personnel who work in prisons and who wish to do more professionally than merely deprive prisoners of their liberty. This concept was often described as rehabilitation, which technically means helping prisoners to put on again the cloak of citizenship.

"A few individuals may be changed for the better by their experiences in prison, but they will always be a small minority and it can be argued that such change comes about despite the prison environment rather than because of it."

The idea of using the prison as a place of reform is likely to be particularly attractive if it can be linked in some way to efforts to reduce crime, but it is very difficult to make any direct connection between the use of imprisonment and national crime rates. In recent years, some jurisdictions have introduced to prisons the target of "reducing recidivism" or "reducing re-offending". If crime is regarded as a series of acts committed by a relatively small, identifiable group of people who are different from the majority of law-abiding citizens, then the objective of changing the behaviour of this small group as a result of their experience in prison should lead to a reduction in the amount of crime that they commit after they are released. If one holds that this small group of people is likely to be responsible for a disproportionate amount of

Finland's Rates of Incarceration

Finland's incarceration rate fell because of policy changes, not because of a reduction in crime rates. Attitudes towards imprisonment have a major effect on imprisonment rates.

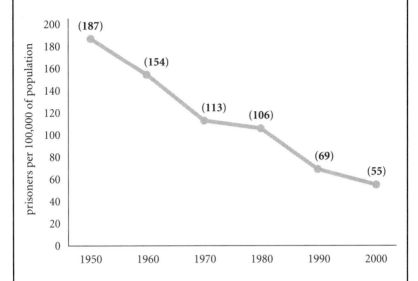

TAKEN FROM: Council of Europe, *European Prison Rules*, Strasbourg, France: Council of Europe Publishing, 2006, p. 106.

crime, then any reduction in their rate of committing crime will in due course lead to an overall reduction in crime. This argument has proved attractive to politicians who need to find a way of responding to public fear of crime.

The general principle that human beings can be encouraged to change their future patterns of behaviour for the better is a sound one but the question of whether this can be achieved in conditions of captivity is very problematic. The reality is that prison is essentially a world set apart from normality. The links which many prisoners have with the social structures, which the rest of us take for granted, are at best tenuous. It is true that in many prisons some staff carry out sterling work in attempting to provide prisoners with opportunities to change themselves and their behaviour. A few individuals may be changed for the better by their experiences in prison, but they will always be a small minority and it can be argued that such change comes about despite the prison environment rather than because of it. In many instances, the best that prison staff can hope to achieve with prisoners is to minimise the negative effects of imprisonment and to help prisoners to use their time in prison to create a personal infrastructure which will help them on release. In the words of the Swedish prison and probation service (KVV):

> There is an unavoidable, built-in contradiction between society's motives for locking away a person and the desire to, at the same time, rehabilitate him to a normal life. Prison shall therefore be formed so as to promote an inmate's readjustment to society and to work against the harmful effects of the deprivation of liberty.

"In the Soviet Union and its allied countries, the main justification for imprisonment was as a means of responding to what was seen as an individual's deviance from the expected unswerving loyalty to the state."

Imprisonment for Public Protection

Another stated purpose of imprisonment is protection of the public from those who commit crime, particularly in a persistent way. This argument is known as incapacitation. In the short term this argument can be valid, particularly as regards public protection in specific neighbourhoods where a significant proportion of crime is being committed by identifiable individuals. However, this type of crime tends to be low level, attracting relatively short prison sentences. The persons concerned may be taken out of the community for a short period of time, but they are likely soon to return. An added problem is that many of the crimes which destabilise communities are not resolved by removing one or two individuals. For example, when small-time drug dealers are removed from a local neighbourhood, it will often be a matter of days, if not hours, before they are replaced by new drug dealers.

There is also an issue of public protection in respect of those people whose behaviour is such that it presents a serious threat to the safety of society. Some of them may already be in prison, convicted of serious crimes, particularly of violence against the person, and still give every indication that, if they were to be released, they would continue to present a real threat to the public. It may well be necessary that these people should be in prison for as long as they present a threat to the public, however long that may be. In any one country the number of people falling into this category is likely to be small. . . .

Imprisonment in the Soviet Union

In the Soviet Union and its allied countries, the main justification for imprisonment was as a means of responding to what was seen as an individual's deviance from the expected unswerving loyalty to the state. The same principle had been employed under the Russian tsar. Imprisonment usually took the form of exile to remote areas where there was a need for labour to exploit natural resources. Later in the Soviet era, economic zones were created specifically to exploit the labour of convicts. As a result the prison system (originally known as Gulag and latterly as Guin) became one of the most important contributors to the Soviet economy.

Following the break up of the Soviet Union this justification for imprisonment was at first weakened and then collapsed in most of the countries involved. This process was accelerated by the accession of central and eastern European countries to the Council of Europe. One consequence of this was that in a number of these countries in the late 1980s and the early 1990s there was a significant reduction in the num-

27

ber of people held in prison. This decrease has continued in some countries, most notably in the Russian Federation, as previously mentioned. However, some of the countries experienced subsequent increases, which continue today. There is room for debate about the extent to which these recent increases have been as a result of these countries adopting, at least in part because of the discussions which have taken place under the auspices of the Council of Europe, the justifications for imprisonment which historically have been used in western Europe, as described above.

New Zealand Prisons Should Be for Rehabilitation, Not Retribution

Catholic Bishops of New Zealand

The Catholic Bishops of New Zealand are entrusted with the spiritual oversight of dioceses in New Zealand. In this viewpoint, the bishops argue that New Zealand's imprisonment rate is unacceptably high. These high rates, the bishops say, do not make people feel safer and are also contrary to the ideals of Christian compassion. The bishops argue that New Zealand should concentrate less on building prisons and seeking retribution and more on supporting victims and rehabilitating criminals.

As you read, consider the following questions:

1. Where does New Zealand rank in rates of imprisonment among developed countries?
2. According to the bishops, how does Finland spend the same amount of money that New Zealand spends on building new prisons?
3. What do the bishops believe should be done with refugees imprisoned while awaiting the outcome of their processes?

Catholic Bishops of New Zealand, "A New Approach, Not New Prisons, Is the Answer to Our Growing Prison Population," The Catholic Church in New Zealand, October 29, 2006. Copyright © 2006 Catholic Communications for the NZ Catholic Bishops' Conference. Reproduced by permission.

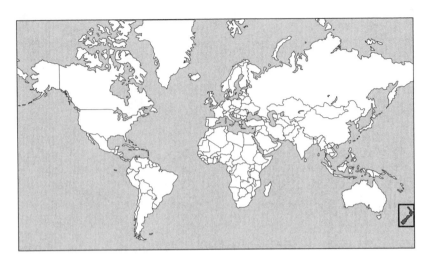

New Zealand has the dubious distinction of having the second highest rate of imprisonment among developed countries. Our rates of incarceration are second only to the United States, where some states reputedly spend more on incarceration than education.

The prison population in New Zealand continues to reach new records, and presently has an imprisonment ratio of 189.7 per 100,000 people, which far exceeds that of other OECD [Organisation for Economic Co-Operation and Development] countries outside the United States.

This has taken place at a time when reported crime, across all categories, is the lowest since 1983. Yet, our imprisonment rate since then has more than doubled, and we continue to build more prisons.

Despite this, most New Zealanders do not feel safer—in fact people fear violent crime more than ever before. Victims of crimes continue to feel unsupported and to have little power or voice in a criminal system aimed at punishment.

Those in prison have fewer and fewer opportunities for rehabilitation. Support services including teachers, psychologists, psychiatrists, social workers and those providing work opportunities and vocational training have all been reduced and even withdrawn. Few prisoners receive access to adequate drug and alcohol treatment programmes or mental health services.

Christ Has Compassion for Prisoners

In the scriptures, we see Christ's compassion both for victims of crime and for those in prisons. Jesus began his ministry with the declaration that he came to set prisoners free. When he speaks of the final judgement, he identifies himself completely with their treatment when he says, "I was a prisoner and you visited me". At the same time the parable of the Good Samaritan tells of the loving care given by a stranger to a victim of crime, and of those who ignored him. Jesus exhorted his followers to follow the example of the one who was "a neighbour" to the man.

The Catholic Church speaks on criminal justice not as a bystander, but as an institution which has made a substantial commitment to victims of crime and those in prisons. Through agencies such as Catholic social services and hospital chaplaincy we assist those who have suffered the results of crime. The Church also provides prison chaplaincy services throughout the country.

"We appeal for a more enlightened approach to the problem of crime, with emphasis on cause and prevention, rather than just apprehension and imprisonment."

For Catholics and other Christians, the message is about repentance, forgiveness and reconciliation rather than calls for retribution and punishment. This is not a soft option. It is an extraordinary task, a difficult and painful path for both victim and offender, requiring an enormous investment of time, resources and support for all parties. But without repentance,

Incarceration Rates of Selected Countries, 2008

Country	Number of Prisoners per 100,000 People
United States	751
Russia	627
Cuba	531
New Zealand	197
Australia	130
Global average	125
Canada	108
Germany	88
Japan	63

TAKEN FROM: *LawFuel.co.nz*, "New Zealand Prison Stats Show New Zealanders Among Most Imprisoned," n.d. [2008]. www.lawfuel.co.nz.

forgiveness and reconciliation, our society risks becoming a more violent and fearful society, creating more victims and more prisoners.

Prisoners themselves need a change of attitude if they are to end their offending and the pain and suffering it causes. But as a prerequisite our society needs a change of attitude. Unless we change our approach to penal policy, our society will continue to become more punitive, judgemental and violent.

Emphasize Prevention, Not Retribution

We appeal for a more enlightened approach to the problem of crime, with emphasis on cause and prevention, rather than just apprehension and imprisonment. Research shows that a retributive and punitive attitude towards offenders is not the answer to solving crime or reducing re-offending. Indeed, it has had the opposite effect.

Prisons must be places where a person is sent as punishment, but always for the purpose of rehabilitation into society. The demand for retribution has a dehumanising and soul-destroying effect on offenders. While we recognize that imprisoning some offenders is necessary for the protection of other people, this is not the sole purpose of prisons. Our prisons must be places where attitudes are corrected. They must be structures which prevent further crime, rather than simply hold prisoners. They must provide opportunities for offenders to address their offending at a personal level, and assist in successful reintegration back into society.

Justice also demands that victims of crime are better supported and compensated than our system provides. In some countries such as Finland the money we spend on building new prisons is spent instead on supporting victims. In New Zealand, however, victims often report that criminal justice proceedings leave them feeling ignored and incidental to the process. With their pain overlooked and their wounds unhealed, they feel left to bear alone the costs of their recovery.

These are not new matters for our society. Almost 20 years ago, the Roper Report [of the Ministerial Committee of Inquiry into Violence] in 1987 warned of an increasingly violent society if we continued along the path of retributive rather than restorative justice.

Ten years ago, we spoke about the same issue: "Too often, offenders repeat their crimes, regardless of the social mayhem this causes. Victims often become embittered and harbour their anger, grief and pain for a lifetime. The community hardens its heart to offenders by demanding longer and harsher penalties. As teachers of the Gospel of Jesus Christ, we hold that compassion, mercy, healing, sanction where appropriate, and forgiveness leading to reconciliation lie at the heart of a fair and just criminal justice system. Even the worst of offenders remain children of God."

Prison Reform Is Vital

In recent months, recommendations have been made by a range of organisations working with prisoners including Prison Fellowship New Zealand and the Salvation Army. We add our voices to theirs, in particular supporting their recommendations:

- That the government initiate a review of the Sentencing Act 2002, the Bail Act 2000 and the Parole Act 2002 with a view to reducing the number of offenders who are remanded or sentenced to prison

- That the government increase the availability of restorative justice-, faith- and cultural-based prison units and other rehabilitative models/pilots with the aim of making these available nationally

- That the government direct the Department of Corrections to develop a plan that will enable all inmates to be actively involved in employment and/or vocational training by the year 2010.

> *"Over the past decade our society has demanded harsher sentences and treatment of those in prisons. In an increasingly violent cycle, both the violence of offenders and the pain and suffering caused to victims have increased."*

In addition we call for a re-examination of the approach taken to people seeking refugee status in New Zealand who are routinely imprisoned while awaiting the outcome of their processes. They should be freed immediately, with appropriate conditions, if they pose no direct threat to national security.

Over the past decade our society has demanded harsher sentences and treatment of those in prisons. In an increasingly violent cycle, both the violence of offenders and the pain and suffering caused to victims have increased and will continue to grow. We cannot afford to continue in this direction.

In Mexico, Violence Is Eroding Catholic Attitudes Toward Punishment

Louis Nevaer

Louis Nevaer is a journalist and writer. In the following viewpoint, he argues that Mexican people have traditionally subscribed to Catholic beliefs suggesting the possibility of redemption for everyone including criminals. As a result, the Mexican justice system has tended to avoid instituting final punishments such as life imprisonment or the death penalty. There has also been reluctance to extradite criminals to other nations, where they may face such punishments. Nevaer points out that a wave of drug-related violence and civilian deaths, however, has led Mexicans to call for harsher punishments including life imprisonment and the death penalty.

As you read, consider the following questions:

1. According to Louis Nevaer, 2008 was the bloodiest year in Mexican history since what event?
2. Will Mexico now extradite individuals facing life imprisonment?
3. What is the longest sentence that Mexican judges typically contemplate?

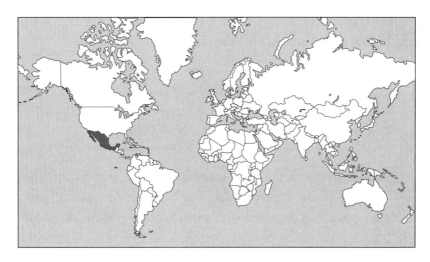

More than twice as many people have been killed in organized crime slayings in Mexico this year than in 2007, making 2008 the bloodiest year in Mexican history since the Mexican Revolution in 1917.

Mexican attorney general Eduardo Medina Mora told reporters this week [December 2008] that drug cartel-related killings rose by 117 percent to 5,376 as compared to the first 11 months of 2007, when there were 2,477 such slayings.

Unprecedented Violence Is Shaking Mexico

"These criminal organizations don't have limits," Mr. Medina Mora, who previously served as Mexico's public safety director, said at a news conference. "They certainly have an enormous power of intimidation."

More Mexicans have been killed in drug-related violence in 2008 than the United States has lost soldiers in five years of conflict in Iraq and Afghanistan. This alarming escalation of violence has shaken Mexico to the core.

Mexican civil society has begun to question the generosity of . . . [its] country's legal system. Mexico has no death penalty, and the maximum prison term—seldom imposed—is 60 years. Additionally, it has refused to extradite individuals facing "cruel and unusual" punishment.

"More Mexicans have been killed in drug-related violence in 2008 than the United States has lost soldiers in five years of conflict in Iraq and Afghanistan."

But the wave of violence that has washed over Mexico this year [2008] is fast transforming the landscape of Mexican society as Mexicans' views on "punishment" are hardening. This shift is not so much because of the violence itself—approximately 92 percent of the 5,400 people killed in Mexico this year were involved in the drug trade—but because innocent civilians are getting caught in the crossfire between the Mexican police and the cartels.

To understand the subtle shifts in attitude, consider how Mexico's views of crime and punishment evolved. Based on the Napoleonic Code introduced in the 19th century—when Napoleon invaded Mexico and installed Maximilian as emperor—Mexico, like most European countries, does not have jury trials and, although there is no presumption of innocence, only "probable" doubt has to be established.

Mexico's legal system reflects Catholic sensibilities: the idea that no one is beyond redemption, that everyone is entitled to forgiveness, and that only God can end a person's life. As a consequence, Mexico has reluctantly extradited people accused of crimes in other countries. Sentences of more than 25 years in prison are seldom imposed, and there is no capital punishment.

American officials have long complained of Mexico's naïveté, arguing that under Mexican law, terrorists can walk free a quarter-century after their crimes. Mexican officials, meanwhile, have argued that with time, people grow and change, and can redeem themselves.

Kidnappings in Mexico

Kidnapping for ransom has become an established criminal business in Mexico with estimates suggesting kidnappers collect over $100 million a year in ransoms. Exact statistics on kidnappings in the country are difficult to determine. Security consultants estimate that between 600 and 3,000 kidnappings occur each year in Mexico....

Mexican officials believe only one-third of all kidnappings are reported to police, largely due to a lack of confidence in authorities or the perception that police officers are members of criminal gangs. Meanwhile, some estimates suggest as little as one-tenth of all kidnappings are reported, as most victims maintain silence even after the ordeal is over, out of fear of repercussions from their abductors if they report the incident to authorities.

Advance Point Global,
"The Kidnappings Threat in Mexico,"
August 1, 2008. http://advancepointglobal.com.

"Mexico's legal system reflects Catholic sensibilities: the idea that no one is beyond redemption, that everyone is entitled to forgiveness, and that only God can end a person's life."

Mexicans Seek Harsher Criminal Penalties

But now that violence—gruesome slayings where mutilated or decapitated bodies are dumped in public view—is affecting ordinary society, Mexico is seeing a public backlash.

As a result, three pillars of the Mexican criminal justice system are under contention:

• *Extradition:* Since taking office in December 2006, President Felipe Calderón has handed over almost 160 criminal suspects to U.S. authorities.

Mexico had long resisted extradition requests on the principle that crimes committed in Mexico should be tried and punished in Mexico. Mexican law, furthermore, made it almost impossible to extradite a person who faced a life sentence or the death penalty. This reluctance began to change during the administration of [Mexican president] Vicente Fox, who sought closer ties to the United States. These efforts were bolstered in 2005 when the Mexican Supreme Court ruled that life sentences did not constitute "cruel" or "unusual" punishment, since the United States "routinely" imposed such sentences. As a consequence, Calderón has moved forcefully to extradite drug suspects indicted in the United States, even if they face life in prison without the possibility of parole; Mexico still refuses to extradite individuals facing the death penalty.

• *Life Sentences:* Mexico's penal code reflects the Catholic belief that no one is beyond redemption. As such, "life imprisonment" is inconsistent with the belief in rehabilitation, and as a result, life sentences in Mexico are considered cruel and unusual punishment. The maximum sentence that a court can impose is 60 years, and this is rarely done; the longest sentence Mexican judges contemplate is 25 years, which they consider long enough for a person to redeem himself or herself.

"Legislators have been inundated with calls for 'concurrent sentences' that would result in prison terms that extend for a person's natural life without the possibility of parole."

But as violence engulfs ordinary citizens, this belief is changing. The rash of kidnappings, particularly of children, has enraged the Mexican public. This, coming after the sensational kidnapping and slaying of Fernando Martí, the 14-year-old son of a sporting goods magnate, has hardened Mexicans' views on life imprisonment.

Felipe Calderón attended the funeral of Fernando Martí, and legislators have been inundated with calls for "concurrent sentences" that would result in prison terms that extend for a person's natural life without the possibility of parole. Reflecting these attitudes, in 2005, Mexico's Supreme Court ruled that "life imprisonment" should no longer be considered "cruel and unusual punishment."

• *Death Penalty:* Perhaps no other aspect of Mexico's penal code reflects a commitment to human rights and religious sensibilities than Mexico's refusal to impose capital punishment. The last person executed in Mexico was in 1961. Mexico is a signatory nation to the U.N.'s Universal Declaration of Human Rights, which forbids executions. In 1981, Mexico signed a human rights treaty as part of the Organization of American States (OAS) that states that capital punishment, once banned, cannot be reintroduced. Mexico continues to refuse to extradite anyone who faces the possibility of the death penalty.

But now, as much out of anger as frustration, Mexicans are debating the merits of capital punishment. Mexican officials have agreed to hold hearings on whether the Constitution should be amended to allow for the death penalty. Humberto Moreira Valdés, governor of the Mexican northern border state of Coahuila, a region engulfed in drug-related violence, sponsored an initiative that would allow capital punishment for convicted kidnappers who kill their victims.

Opponents to the death penalty accuse Valdés of exploiting the public's growing fear with "impossible" initiatives. "Behind this call [for the reintroduction of capital punishment] is society's desperation over the climate of insecurity we are living in," Alberto Herrera, director of the Mexico chapter of Amnesty International, told reporters. "But the risk is it leads to calls for revenge." Although few believe it is possible to change the Mexican Constitution, the simple fact that the question of capital punishment has entered the public debate reflects the heightened sense of outrage—and powerlessness—that ordinary Mexicans feel.

An increasing number of them are beginning to feel that it would be criminal for society to do nothing in the face of crime.

British Crime Rates Would Decrease if Imprisonment Rates Increased

Civitas

Civitas: The Institute for the Study of Civil Society is a British think tank dedicated to deepening public understanding of the legal, institutional, and moral framework that makes a free and democratic society possible. The following viewpoint explains that during the late 1980s and 1990s, the United States increased imprisonment and its crime rates fell; at the same time, England and Wales lowered imprisonment rates and saw crime rates rise. The authors conclude that the British government should increase imprisonment rates to help reduce crime.

As you read, consider the following questions:

1. Was the 1996 U.S. murder rate higher or lower than the 1996 murder rate in England and Wales?

2. In England and Wales, what was the one crime for which a strong link existed between the severity of punishment and the rate of crime?

3. According to Civitas, which two crimes do not seem to decrease when the risk of imprisonment is increased?

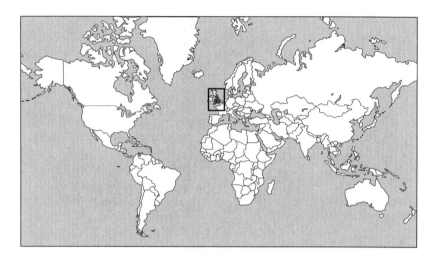

The [British] government has set out to reduce crime, but the evidence from a study comparing the policies pursued in the USA with those in England and Wales suggests it has adopted the wrong policies. From the early 1980s until the mid-1990s the risk of imprisonment increased in the USA and the crime rate fell; while in England and Wales the opposite happened: The risk of imprisonment fell and the crime rate increased. Then, from 1993, policy in England and Wales was reversed and the risk of imprisonment increased, though it remained historically low. Even this relatively small increase in the use of prison was followed by a reduction in crime.

The United States Has More Imprisonment and Less Crime

A study carried out by one of Britain's most distinguished criminologists, Professor David Farrington of the University of Cambridge, in conjunction with Patrick Langan of the US Department of Justice, compared the USA with England and Wales between 1981 and 1996. Crime rates based on crime surveys were available in both countries up to 1995, and crime figures based on police records to 1996. The study investigated the possibility that increasing the risk of punishment would lead to falling crime. Two measures of the risk of punishment were used: the conviction rate per 1,000 alleged offenders and the incarceration rate per 1,000 alleged offenders. . . .

The original study by Langan and Farrington was published in 1998 and gives imprisonment rates and crime rates in England and Wales based on the British Crime Survey [BCS] up to 1995. The 1997 BCS results were not available and so the study does not fully capture the impact of the policy reversal in 1993. However, Professor Farrington and Darrick Jolliffe have subsequently updated the estimates for England and Wales to 1999, allowing us to appraise the impact of the policy reversal. This study is not yet published [as of 2003], and we are very grateful to them for permitting us to quote from it.

"The study found that the chances of being imprisoned increased *in the USA between 1981 and 1995 and* fell *in England and Wales. During the same period, crime* fell *in the USA and* increased *in England and Wales."*

The original 1998 comparison showed that the USA and England and Wales pursued very different policies and produced very different results. The study found that the chances of being imprisoned *increased* in the USA between 1981 and 1995 and *fell* in England and Wales. During the same period, crime *fell* in the USA and *increased* in England and Wales.

From 1981 to 1995 (1994 for the USA), an offender's risk of being caught, convicted, and sentenced to custody increased in the United States for all six crimes in the study (murder, rape, robbery, assault, burglary, and motor vehicle theft) but fell in England and Wales for all except murder. For example, in the US in 1981 there were 13 imprisoned robbers for every 1,000 alleged robbers. By 1994 there were 17. In England and Wales, there were 7 imprisoned robbers for every 1,000 alleged robbers in 1981, and only 4 in 1995. There were 5.5 impris-

45

oned burglars for every 1,000 alleged burglars in the US, increasing to 8.4 in 1994. In England and Wales there were 7.8 in 1981 and only 2.2 in 1995. . . .

What happened to the crime rate during this period? According to the 1995 victim surveys, rates of robbery, assault, burglary, and motor vehicle theft were all higher in England and Wales than [in] the United States. According to 1996 police statistics, crime rates were higher in England and Wales for three crimes: assault, burglary, and motor vehicle theft. In the US in 1996 there were 9.4 burglaries for every 1,000 population, compared with 22.4 in England and Wales; and there were 5.3 car thefts per 1,000 population in the US compared with 9.5 in England and Wales. . . .

The major exception to the trend is the murder rate. The 1996 US murder rate was nearly six times higher than the rate in England and Wales, although the difference between the two countries narrowed from 1981 to 1996. Guns were more frequently used in violent crimes in the United States than in England and Wales. According to 1996 police statistics, firearms were used in 68% of US murders and in 7% of English and Welsh murders, and in 41% of US robberies but only 5% of English and Welsh robberies.

The overall US crime rate—whether measured by surveys of crime victims or by police statistics—was lower in 1996 than in 1981. In the US, for assault, burglary, and motor vehicle theft (according to victim surveys) and murder, robbery, and burglary (according to police records) the rates in 1996 were the lowest recorded in the 16-year period from 1981 to 1996. By comparison, English and Welsh crime rates in 1995 (as measured by the BCS) and 1996 (based on police statistics) were higher than they had been in 1981.

How large were the differences between 1981 and 1996? And how did they change during the period studied?

- The US robbery rate as measured in the victim survey was nearly double that in England and Wales in 1981, but in 1995 the English and Welsh robbery rate was 1.4 times America's.

- The English and Welsh assault rate as measured by the victim survey was slightly higher than America's in 1981, but in 1995 the English and Welsh assault rate was more than double America's.

- The US burglary rate as measured by the victim survey was more than double that in England and Wales in 1981, but in 1995 the English and Welsh burglary rate was nearly double America's.

- The English and Welsh motor vehicle theft rate as measured in the victim survey was 1.5 times America's in 1981, but in 1995 the English and Welsh rate for vehicle theft was more than double America's.

- The US murder rate as measured in police statistics was 8.7 times that in England and Wales in 1981 but 5.7 times higher in 1996.

- The US rape rate as measured in police statistics was 17 times that in England and Wales in 1981, but 3 times greater in 1996.

Criminals Faced Decreased Risk of Punishment

Langan and Farrington found that in England and Wales in the early 1990s, criminals faced a lower risk of punishment compared with the USA. Moreover, the risk had fallen between 1981 and 1995. Why did the risk of punishment fall in England and Wales and increase in the US? The study suggests three causes of diminishing conviction rates in England and Wales. First, there was an increased use of cautions and unrecorded warnings. (This policy has subsequently been changed for young offenders.) Second, the Police and Criminal Evidence Act of 1984 increased the procedural safeguards for the accused. And third, the Crown Prosecution Service [a government prosecution office, replacing prosecutions by police] was established in 1986, leading to an increased tendency to drop cases.

Two special factors caused the decreasing risk of prison from 1987–1991. First, official home office advice encouraged judges to make less use of prison and second, theft of a motor vehicle was downgraded in 1988 to a non-indictable offence encouraging the use of non-custodial sentences.

From 1993, however, home office policy changed and the use of prison was encouraged, especially for repeat offenders, although the rate of imprisonment remained low compared with the US. In the US, however, during the same period, the police made more arrests as a percentage of total alleged offenders and prosecutors obtained more convictions. And, after 1986, US prisoners served a longer percentage of their sentences.

"In England and Wales in the early 1990s, criminals faced a lower risk of punishment compared with the USA."

Severity of Sentencing Is Less Important in Reducing Crime

In addition to examining the impact of changes in the risk of punishment on the crime rate, Langan and Farrington also looked at the impact of changes in the severity of punishment. Four measures of severity were used: the proportion of those convicted who were sent to prison; length of the sentence; actual time served; and the percentage of the sentence served. . . .

A negative correlation between the risk of punishment and the rate of crime was taken as support for the theory that an increased risk of punishment leads to a fall in crime. In England and Wales they found strong support for the theory that 'links falling risk of punishment to rising crime'. After 1981 the conviction rate in England and Wales fell and the crime rate (whether based on victim surveys or police records) rose. Similarly, the incarceration rate fell and the crime rate rose. However, the correlations between the severity of punishment and the crime rate were mixed. There was, however, a strong link between the severity of punishment of car thieves and the rate of vehicle theft. After 1981, the proportion of car thieves sentenced to prison, their average sentence, the time served and the percentage of sentence served, as well as the number of days of actual incarceration, all fell. During this time, vehicle theft rose, according to both the British Crime Survey and police records.

"Overall, this evidence is consistent with the theory that the important factor in reducing crime is the risk of imprisonment rather than the severity of the sentence."

Was it the greater risk of punishment that explains the difference in crime rates in England and Wales at the end of the period? Or was it the severity of sentencing? Sentences were likely to be longer in the US. For all offences (murder, rape, robbery, assault, burglary, motor vehicle theft), courts in the United States sentenced convicted offenders to longer periods of incarceration than courts in England and Wales, and the length of time actually served before being released was also longer in the United States than in England and Wales. However, over the period, sentences for serious crimes generally did not *increase* in length in the United States, while in England and Wales sentences generally did get somewhat longer for the three violent crimes, murder, rape and robbery. Over-

49

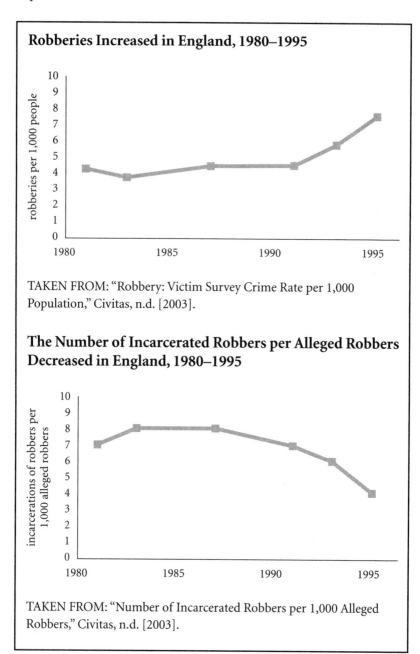

Robberies Increased in England, 1980–1995

TAKEN FROM: "Robbery: Victim Survey Crime Rate per 1,000 Population," Civitas, n.d. [2003].

The Number of Incarcerated Robbers per Alleged Robbers Decreased in England, 1980–1995

TAKEN FROM: "Number of Incarcerated Robbers per 1,000 Alleged Robbers," Civitas, n.d. [2003].

all, this evidence is consistent with the theory that the important factor in reducing crime is the risk of imprisonment rather than the severity of the sentence as such. . . .

Alternatives to Prison Are Less Effective

Is the [prime minister Tony] Blair government pursuing the right policies? The government is ambiguous about prison. In its 2002 white paper, *Justice for All*, it says that it wants to send the 'strongest possible message' to criminals that the system will be effective in 'detecting, convicting and properly punishing them'. So far so good: After many years of being opposed to prison and favouring community sentences, the government now recognises that prison protects the public more effectively. But prison is to be reserved for 'dangerous, serious and seriously persistent offenders and those who have consistently breached community sentences'. For the bulk of criminals, the government still hopes to find alternatives to prison that combine community and custodial sentences including weekend prison and more intensive supervision by the [National] Probation Service. Moreover, the use of the term '*seriously* persistent offender' rather than just plain 'persistent offender' suggests that criminals serving community sentences will be allowed to commit more than one offence before being sent to jail.

Comparison of the policies pursued in the US and England and Wales suggests that the strategy outlined in *Justice for All* is unlikely to achieve its intended purpose. For crimes such as robbery, burglary, car theft and assault, increasing the risk of imprisonment has produced a fall in crime in the USA. It appears to be less effective for murder and rape and we may conjecture that this is because the motives or emotional drives leading to these offences are less subject to rational calculation. Where the crimes are calculated to acquire material possessions, potential offenders may be more likely to weigh up the risk of being punished. People addicted to drugs are an exception—but it is a truism to say that they are not likely to be thinking clearly, precisely because they have fallen under the sway of a narcotic substance.

The Blair government is actively promoting alternatives to prison, a strategy that may well be seen as weakening the risk of punishment. Two effects led to the fall in crime in America. First, there was a deterrent effect and second, an incapacitation effect. It is clear from the evidence set out so far that the government's proposals are likely to weaken the deterrent effect, because criminals will be aware that they face a lower risk of imprisonment. But, in addition, the proposals will also weaken the incapacitation effect, because more offenders will be at large rather than in custody. A criminal cannot commit offences in the wider society while he is in prison, but a person under a community sentence can. The government partly acknowledges this weakness and plans to overcome it by increasing the level of supervision of offenders in the community—under intensive supervision and surveillance programmes. However, the greater the time spent unsupervised, the longer the time offenders will have available for crime. And, however tough sounding the language used to describe community sentences, it is an inescapable fact that the government is increasing the amount of time known offenders will be unsupervised. They may be required to attend a training course or to go to work during the working day, and they may be tagged from 7:00 P.M. until 7:00 A.M., but this leaves them free to carry out crimes on the way home from work or college.

"A criminal cannot commit offences in the wider society while he is in prison, but a person under a community sentence can."

Prison Can Punish, Protect, and Rehabilitate

Prison works as a method of protecting the public and deterring criminals, but some commentators are reluctant to accept the truth of this conclusion because they feel that punishment and the rehabilitation of offenders are mutually exclusive alternatives. Prison is certainly a punishment, but it is not *only* a punishment. It is also a means of protecting the public from known offenders and of deterring others. It is also—as the Prison Service fully acknowledges—an opportunity to reform criminals in the hope of encouraging a law-abiding lifestyle on release. And, as the Prison Service freely admits, efforts to reform prisoners are much in need of improvement. Measures intended to rehabilitate offenders while they are in custody need to be quickly and substantially stepped up. Much has been learnt about how to discourage antisocial attitudes, to create a stronger moral sense, and to encourage a more positive attitude in convicted criminals. But while their offending continues, it is preferable to rehabilitate them in prison, so that members of the public continue to be protected.

The evidence produced by this comparison of America and England and Wales suggests that, to the extent that it is reducing the risk of punishment and decreasing the supervision of known offenders, the Blair government is doing the opposite of what is necessary to reduce crime.

Prison Should Be Abolished

Peter Collins, Joint Effort, Julia Sudbury, Kim Pate, Patricia Monture, and Caitlin Hewitt-White

In this viewpoint, interviewer Caitlin Hewitt-White asks various prison activists in Canada and the United States their views on prison reform. They all agree that prison reform is problematic, since improving prison conditions can actually strengthen or expand the prison system as a whole. For example, one author says that expanding mental health facilities in prisons has led to placing more of the mentally ill behind bars for treatment. The writers argue that improving the lives of prisoners is important for the short term, but the long-term goal should always be complete abolition of prisons.

As you read, consider the following questions:

1. Why does Julia Sudbury suggest she would not support hospice care within prisons?
2. In what country is the Holloway Prison for women located?
3. According to Patricia Monture, what do those outside of the criminal justice system take comfort in thinking?

*C*aitlin Hewitt-White: How far do we go with making prisons better places to live? What, in particular, is the revolutionary potential of prison reform, if any?

Peter Collins, Joint Effort, Julia Sudbury, Kim Pate, Patricia Monture, and Caitlin Hewitt-White, "Prison Abolition in Canada," *Upping the Anti: A Journal of Theory and Action Online*, vol. 7, October 2007. Reproduced by permission.

Peter Collins: I think it's a rare and short-sighted prisoner who covets a prettier and nicer prison. It's imperative that we demand proper physical and mental health care for prisoners while in the long term do strategic work, moving forward to enlighten society about the caustic and destructive nature of prison, no matter how modern the facility.

It's highly unlikely that we'll ever see a revolution in our time. The revolution will have to be an evolution. Society is currently apathetic about the issues. They have bought into the premise that the state's current response is the only safe measure against the scourge of criminality and mayhem washing over our continent. Education is the only thing that works, and it'll have to be a multi-prong approach with very long-term goals.

Prison Reform Is Not Revolutionary

Joint Effort: This question was difficult to answer and we must admit to having serious doubts about the revolutionary potential of prison reform. As part of our work, we continually struggle with issues of cooperation with the prison system (with the risk of co-option and complicity) versus non-cooperation, which may be more desirable but really only viable once our abolition movement gets reasonably strong, both inside and out.

Ultimately, the goal should not be to make prisons a better place to live, but to challenge their existence. For now, this means that we are as careful as we can be when deciding where, when and how to respond to prisoners' requests/needs. We always ask, "What is this demand going to achieve? Who benefits and whose interests are being served?" In this way, every struggle for change in the fight for prisoners' rights can have as its short-term objective better conditions for those still inside. The important thing is that reforms are never sought as an end in and of themselves, but rather as evidence of our (prisoner and activists) experiences and efforts to raise public awareness of the issues and further our efforts towards abolishing prisons.

"Ultimately, the goal should not be to make prisons a better place to live, but to challenge their existence."

Improving Conditions Is Important, but Not Enough

Julia Sudbury: As long as the prison justice movement involves prisoner leadership, it will always include campaigns to improve the immediate living conditions of prisoners. People are dying preventable deaths in prison and face immense mental and physical pain. Obviously we have to challenge the conditions that cause this. At the same time, we do need to be wary of getting sidetracked into helping the state to improve its prisons, at the expense of decarcerative [removal of people from prison] work.

In the prison abolitionist movement, we talk about "non-reformist reforms." In other words, we think through the strategies that we are promoting for immediate small-scale changes in terms of whether they support or undermine the long-term goal of a world without prisons. This means that we may not support the construction of hospice care [care for people near the end of their lives] within prisons, for example, because it undermines the bid to get elderly and terminally ill prisoners released to the community.

In my opinion, any organization dedicated to improving conditions for prisoners must either support abolition as a long-term strategy, or accept that they are strengthening the prison-industrial complex and ultimately leading to more and more people's lives being destroyed.

Prisoners Should Be Called Prisoners

"Prisoner" is the only correct term to describe a person locked into a cage or cell within a facility not of one's choice and whose quality of existence therein depends upon the keeper(s). Not "inmate"—an inpatient of a mental hospital who may or may not have voluntarily entered the "institution." Not "client"—a person who has purchased the services of a chosen deliverer, is a patron of the one hired and/or is an outpatient—someone who chooses to be a client. The term "resident" is also an obvious corruption.

"Prisoner" is the only correct term. Never "offender"—the continual use of the term "offender" justifies everything done to "an inmate in the name of the law." Yet "offender" describes a person who commits an offence—a current transgression, one that is occurring at a specific time. Charged with an offence, the person is tried, and if convicted becomes a prisoner. The offence has already happened. It is in the past. The prisoner in prison is not offending. S/he has already offended. S/he may have "offended" once and may never "offend" again, but utilizing the label, "offender" permits an ongoing and static reference justifying brutalization and degradation (euphemistically referred to as "treatment of the offender") and enables the continuum of power distinctions.

Canadian Association of Elizabeth Fry Societies,
"Guidelines for Advocacy." www.elizabethfry.ca.

Improving Conditions May Lead to More Prisoners

Kim Pate: Well, I'm not in favor of anybody having a horrible experience anywhere. On the other hand, improving prisons is a bit of a fool's game. Mental health is a good example. We saw progressive trends in mental health several decades ago when people moved into the community, not always as well-resourced as they should be, but "normalization" and "deinstitutionalization" approaches were important and positive trends. In Canada and the US, especially since the drastic evisceration of the social safety net in the mid-90s, people who had historically been dependent on that net became overrepresented in prisons. Not surprisingly, the only system left to support these socially marginalized people is the criminal justice system.

Because of cuts to mental health services, people with "mental health issues" and mental disabilities are coming into the system. The policy of providing more mental health services in women's prisons was not necessarily ill-conceived. But the reality is that these new "mental health services" in prisons are always annexed to prisons. In fact, the mental health component is always secondary to the process of criminalization. Behavior that used to be seen as symptomatic of a woman's mental health is now more likely to be seen through the lens of criminalization. Paradoxically, the federal corrections system has committed $30 million in five years to mental health services, but at the very least it's going to exacerbate the problem for those individuals who are already in the system. Likely it will be linked to more people being sent to prison because the perception amongst judges, many lawyers and many members of the public is that the only way now to get mental health services to a criminalized or marginalized person is to send them to prison. Leaving the system becomes an increasingly remote reality. Prison is one of the few places where there are resources being pumped into mental health services. People are being given longer sentences under the guise of treatment.

The corrections system can argue that women have access to some of the best prison services, but obviously, this type of thinking is flawed. Even the "best" prison services are failing them. Extricating young women from the system is going to be increasingly challenging because everything that will help them survive if they were to be released into the community—services, support, a social safety net—is being systematically attacked. This helps create the illusion that their ability to become "self-reliant" and "healthy" is possible only in a prison environment. Young women actually become less self-reliant in a prison, less able to resist, and less able to thrive in a community if and when they get back there, and too many of them die in the process.

"The perception amongst judges, many lawyers and many members of the public is that the only way now to get mental health services to a criminalized or marginalized person is to send them to prison. . . . People are being given longer sentences under the guise of treatment."

I joined my current paid work after our organization had gone through what was seen internationally as one of the most progressive and far-reaching prison reform efforts, the Task Force on Federally Sentenced Women. Half of the members were community members, as well as a number of Aboriginal women. The task force seemed to promote a whole new approach to working with women inside, but what we ended up seeing was an appropriation of our language and a bastardization of our recommendations. While I was an abolitionist before joining, this experience very clearly led our organization to taking an abolitionist perspective, a vision of "Canada without prisons," as our mission statement now reads. It was very clear the minute the report was done and the framework was put in place that even those well-intentioned and committed bureaucrats had to go about the business of systematically appropriating the language and bastardizing the approaches. I've spoken to people in other parts of [the] world where similar reform approaches have led to similar results. In Britain there were great reform efforts planned for the Holloway Prison for women, and now all the women that were involved in that are abolitionists. We all recognize that the best prisons in the world are no prisons.

Prisoners Should Set the Agenda for Prison Reform

Patricia Monture: Well, I don't think that's a question that somebody like me can decide, because there are people who live in those places, and inhumane things are going on, and I don't think I have some kind of a right to choose for them. I participated in the Task Force on Federally Sentenced Women solely because the Aboriginal women at the prison for women asked me to. If they hadn't asked me to, I wouldn't have gone ahead and done that. I think that part of our activism around the prisoner justice movement has to come from living by example. We have to turn the power we have as unsentenced people over to the prisoners. You don't get to decide what happens, they do. They're the ones who are living it. I think that prisoners have to decide what is "tolerable," but that also feels like a crazy way to think.

> *"We have to turn the power we have as unsentenced people over to the prisoners. You don't get to decide what happens, they do. They're the ones who are living it."*

Is there a revolutionary potential in prison reform? No. There's no revolutionary potential at all because that system is so wrong—that system of having power over. Many of the things that we thought when we talked in the past about empowering women we meant in a very systemic and structural kind of way. We weren't talking about empowering individual women. We were talking about equality. We were talking about doing something about the rape and violence against women in society. That's what I think empowerment meant to me at the time. That's been flipped over into this idea that women have to individually take responsibility for the crimes they commit. It's been turned into this notion of "risk," which gets applied today with regularity.

So, do I think there's a revolutionary potential in prison reform? Absolutely not. I think prison is an absolutely crazy idea. Part of the problem is that the prison is seen as serving a social good. Everyone who doesn't have any involvement with the criminal justice system takes comfort in thinking "those people over there, the bad people, the criminals, they're all in jail. Gee, that must mean I'm good." I mean, that's drastically oversimplified, but that's basically what is going on. To me that's a crazy way to keep social order. That's why prison abolition is so important. My view now, based on what I've learned in my life, is that you can't fix something that's just a wrong idea from the get-go. You can't fix the place.

Periodical Bibliography

Theodore Dalrymple
"Finally—An Admission That Prison Does Work," *Times Online*, December 7, 2007. www.timesonline.co.uk.

Jamie Doward
"Jail Doesn't Work, Say Crime Victims," *Guardian*, August 13, 2006.

FOX News
"Mexico Outraged by Killing of Anti-Crime Activist," July 9, 2009. www.foxnews.com.

David G. Green
"Crime Is Falling—Because Prison Works," *Guardian*, July 20, 2003.

Nick Herbert
"The Abolitionists' Criminal Conspiracy," *Guardian*, July 27, 2008.

Independent
"Prison Doesn't Work. So Why Are We Locking Up So Many People?" March 2, 2002.

PhysOrg.com
"Study: Potential Criminals Deterred by Longer Sentences," May 18, 2009. www.physorg.com.

Michael Santos
"Warehousing vs. Rehabilitation as the Goal of Prison," Prison News Blog, March 26, 2009. http://prisonnewsblog.com.

Stratfor
"Organized Crime in Mexico," March 11, 2008. www.stratfor.com.

Tamara Walsh
"Is Corrections Correcting? An Examination of Prisoner Rehabilitation Policy and Practice in Queensland," *Australian and New Zealand Journal of Criminology*, April 2006.

Don Weatherburn, Jiuzhao Hua, and Steve Moffatt
"How Much Crime Does Prison Stop? The Incapacitation Effect of Prison on Burglary," *Crime and Justice Bulletin*, no. 93, January 2006.

James Q. Wilson
"What Do We Get from Prison?" The Volokh Conspiracy, June 9, 2008. http://volokh.com.

GLOBALVIEWPOINTS

CHAPTER 2

Sentencing and Imprisonment

Life Imprisonment May Violate Human Rights

Dirk van Zyl Smit

Dirk van Zyl Smit is a professor of comparative and international penal law at the University of Nottingham, an advocate of the High Court of South Africa, and the author of Taking Life Imprisonment Seriously in National and International Law *(2002). In this viewpoint, van Zyl Smit points out that some nations such as Germany have concluded that in denying the possibility of reformation, a life sentence violates human rights. Worldwide, however, life sentences remain less controversial than the death penalty, and van Zyl Smit explains that little effective international opposition to life sentences exists.*

As you read, consider the following questions:

1. What is the notion of the *Behandlungsvollzug?*
2. What two European constitutional courts have adopted the same view of life imprisonment as their German counterpart?
3. According to Dirk van Zyl Smit, the historical roots of the complete prohibition on life sentences can be traced to the criminal law theory of what country?

Dirk van Zyl Smit, "Life Imprisonment: Recent Issues in National and International Law," *International Journal of Law and Psychiatry*, vol. 29, no. 5, September–October 2006, pp. 405–406, 408–412. Copyright © 2006 Elsevier B.V. All rights reserved. Reproduced with permission from Elsevier, conveyed through Copyright Clearance Center, Inc.

Unlike the death penalty, which is always hugely controversial, life imprisonment only occasionally surfaces as a headline-making issue of criminal policy. A primary reason for this is that not only in the public mind, but also in the specialist understanding of penologists, there is often considerable ambiguity about what life imprisonment means. This ambiguity was well captured . . . by Lord [Michael] Mustill [a British Judge]. . .:

> The sentence of life imprisonment is also unique in that the words, which the judge is required to pronounce, do not mean what they say. Whilst in a very small minority of cases the prisoner is in the event confined for the rest of his natural life, this is not the usual or intended effect of a sentence of life imprisonment. . . . But although everyone knows what the words do not mean, nobody knows what they do mean, since the duration of the prisoner's detention depends on a series of recommendations . . . and executive decisions. . . .

Life Sentences Are Poorly Understood

Lord Mustill's words may well be an accurate reflection of both public and specialist opinion on the subject, but if they are to be applied internationally they need two major qualifications: First, it is by no means true everywhere that life sentences, even those imposed on children, will lead to eventual release. Secondly, even where there are procedures for considering the release of prisoners sentenced to life imprisonment, not everyone will accept that they are sufficient, either in theory or in practice, to make life sentences a form of punishment that meets the requirements of human rights standards as developed by international law and national constitutions.

In order to reflect the complexity of life sentence, this article will consider, in the light of these two qualifications, various controversies that have emerged surrounding life imprisonment in recent years. It is not an exhaustive survey but rather gives illustrative examples of recent arguments and trends. The focus is on formal sentences of life imprisonment, although some attention is paid to other forms of indefinite detention that might amount to life sentences in practice. . . .

"It is by no means true everywhere that life sentences, even those imposed on children, will lead to eventual release."

Life Imprisonment Should Include Treatment

Is it possible to deny adults the possibility of eventual reformation? If not, what are the implications of this for the death penalty? This issue was at the core of a fascinating debate about life imprisonment that played itself out in the German Federal Constitutional Court in the 1970s and which is of general interest at the European level where the issue of whether a whole life sentence is acceptable for an adult who has committed a truly heinous offence is still unresolved.

The matter arose in the famous life imprisonment case of the German Federal Constitutional Court of 21 June 1977. In that case the court was asked to rule on the fundamental question, namely whether a life sentence *per se* was constitutional. The bald conclusion to which the Federal Constitutional Court came was that the sentence of life imprisonment for murder was not inherently unconstitutional. However, its wide-ranging judgment covered most of the debate about life imprisonment and its recommendations had an important impact on subsequent practical developments in Germany. The key to its reasoning was its acceptance of the notion of the *Behandlungsvollzug*, that is of the treatment-orientated implementation of the sentence of imprisonment, and its enthusiastic endorsement of the then new Prison Act as the legal vehicle for this policy. As the Court expressed it:

The threat of life imprisonment is complemented, as is constitutionally required, by meaningful treatment of the prisoner. The prison institutions also have the duty in the case of prisoners sentenced to life imprisonment, to strive towards their resocialization, to preserve their ability to cope with life and to counteract the negative effects of incarceration and destructive personality changes that go with it. . . .

This understanding of the function of the prison system assisted the court in rejecting the submission that life imprisonment necessarily leads to prisoners suffering permanent psychological damage. . . .

"In German law there could be no life sentences without the prospect of eventual release."

A Life Sentence Is Acceptable When Release Is Possible

At the same time, the positive attitude adopted by the Federal Constitutional Court towards reformation, what it called resocialization, made it more sympathetic to the view that the manner in which prisoners serving life sentences should be released should be reconsidered. The court held that life imprisonment could only be regarded as compatible with human dignity . . . if the prisoner retained a concrete and fundamentally realizable expectation of eventually being released:

> The essence of human dignity is attacked if the prisoner, notwithstanding his personal development, must abandon any hope of ever regaining his freedom.

Simply stated, the German court recognised that this fundamental principle applied to all human beings. . . . In German law there could be no life sentences without the prospect of eventual release. . . .

The question of whether a life without parole sentence meets human rights norms has not been finally settled in Europe. Constitutional courts in France and Italy have adopted the same view as their German counterpart and ruled that whole life sentences are fundamentally unacceptable. On the other hand, the House of Lords in England has held that such a sentence would be acceptable in principle. It stated explicitly that "there are cases where the crimes are so wicked that even if the prisoner is detained until he or she dies it will not exhaust the requirements of retribution and deterrence". . . .

At some stage the European Court of Human Rights (ECHR) will have to decide this issue. While questions may arise at the European level about the adequacy of the envisaged release procedures for these prisoners, the crucial question will be whether a sentence that denies prisoners a formal prospect of release is fundamentally an inhuman or degrading punishment and thus contrary to Article 3 of the European Convention on Human Rights. . . .

The distinction between whole life sentences that may infringe fundamental human rights and life sentences for serious offences where there is a procedure for release that do not, once again highlights the ambiguity about what is really meant by life sentences. It points to the need for exploring whether such procedures can meet the requirement of due process and can give lifers a realistic prospect of regaining their freedom.

Before doing so it is necessary, however, to consider a more radical critique of life imprisonment in a number of jurisdictions. This approach has resulted in their jurisprudence fundamentally opposing life imprisonment in all its forms.

In Many Countries, Life Imprisonment Is Never Acceptable

There are several countries in the world in which no form of life imprisonment is a sentencing option. In some of them— Portugal, Brazil, Costa Rica, Columbia, El Salvador are examples—the national constitution explicitly outlaws its imposition. In others the Constitutional Court has declared life imprisonment to be unconstitutional: In both Mexico and Peru there have recently been such decisions. Finally, in a third group, the legislature has chosen without direct constitutional compulsion not to provide for life imprisonment in the criminal code. Spain, Norway and latterly Slovenia are examples of this last group.

"While in Germany the Constitutional Court upheld life imprisonment as a form of punishment subject to adequate release procedures being put in place, in these countries the constitutional courts outlawed the penalty in its entirety."

The historical roots of this prohibition can be traced to a humanitarian view of punishment that has its roots in 19th century Portuguese criminal law theory in particular: Portugal outlawed life imprisonment as early as 1884, although its constitutional prohibition is more modern. This humanitarian approach is often combined with a specific injunction found in the constitutions of many of these states, that imprisonment should have a 're-educative' function. Spanish scholars in particular have argued that this constitutional requirement means that life imprisonment is unacceptable, for the sentence raises the possibility, at very least, that the offender will never be returned to society and therefore there is the risk that the success of the re-education that is supposed to happen in prison will never be put to the test. It is this argument that appears to have persuaded the constitutional courts of Mexico and Peru to declare life imprisonment unconstitutional.

The logic of the argument is substantially the same as the one that was advanced against life imprisonment in Germany. However, the difference in outcome is significant: While in Germany the Constitutional Court upheld life imprisonment

Life Without Parole Worldwide

Hardening sentencing practices and the pressure for 'truth in sentencing' has resulted in the increased prevalence of offenders being sentenced to life imprisonment without the possibility of release, or life without parole [LWOP]. It has also been introduced in countries following the abolition of the death penalty. Sentences amounting to LWOP are currently applied in all regions of the world including in Bulgaria, Estonia, the Netherlands, Sweden, Turkey, UK, Ukraine, US, and Vietnam. Whilst in Vietnam amnesties are usually granted after the prisoner has served between 20 and 30 years, other countries' policies are more severe. In Turkey, LWOP sentences passed under their anti-terrorism law do not provide for the possibility of release under any circumstances. In the Netherlands, prisoners have the opportunity to apply for parole but it can be granted only by royal decree and is rarely applied. Similarly, in Estonia, the president may grant clemency but has not done so since the country's independence from the former USSR.

Penal Reform International,
Alternatives to the Death Penalty, *2007.*

as a form of punishment subject to adequate release procedures being put in place, in these countries the constitutional courts outlawed the penalty in its entirety. The reason for the different outcome is not apparent. It can possibly be found in the preexisting scepticism in the Spanish- and Portuguese-speaking world towards life imprisonment on the libertarian grounds that it gave the state too much power over the individual. A further reason may be the fact that sentences of life imprisonment are not imposed in these countries at all.

Life Terms Are Acceptable Internationally

A particularly interesting aspect of the principled opposition to life imprisonment is the lack of success that states that adopt this position have had in maintaining it when other states are involved. One example is in the debate about what form the ultimate penalty that could be imposed by the new international criminal court should take. Although South American members of the International Law Commission in particular had raised principled objections to life imprisonment in the debate about ultimate penalties that arose when the Draft Code of Crimes Against the Peace and Security of Mankind was being considered in the 1990s, and although similar concerns were expressed by national representatives of Portugal and Brazil when the Statute of the International Criminal Court was being finalised in Rome in 1998, life imprisonment duly became the ultimate penalty that the International Criminal Court could impose. . . .

"While a condition that the death penalty must not be imposed is usually honoured, in the case of the life sentence, argument about what 'life' really means allows the issue of principle to be fudged."

A second example of the relative powerlessness of states that prohibit life imprisonment occurs in the areas of extradition. On the face of it this should not be a difficulty. Some treaties allow extradition to be refused if the person to be extradited may be punished not only by the death penalty but also by life imprisonment. . . .

Even where there is no specific reference to life imprisonment in an extradition treaty between two countries, the requested state ought still to be able to stipulate that it will only allow extradition if the persons to be extradited will not face a penalty that would be unconstitutional in the state from which his extradition is being sought. A wide-ranging recent study of extradition practice between the United States of America, as a country seeking extradition, and Mexico and other South and Central American states whose constitutions prohibit life imprisonment, shows that this is often not the case. What happens in practice is that in some instances conditions that life imprisonment should not be imposed are not set, even where the constitution of the extraditing state would appear to require such a condition. In other instances such conditions are set but simply ignored by United States courts. More subtly, the conditions may be ambiguous, or be interpreted as such. For example, the condition may be only that the state will not seek a life sentence but will deliberately omit to mention that an independent court may still impose such a sentence. On other occasions the problem is simply avoided by imposing a very long fixed-term sentence, which is a life sentence in all but name. Once again *Realpolitik* [politics based on practical considerations rather than ethical or ideological objections] has much to do with the downplaying of principled objections to life imprisonment. In the United States there have been various attempts to pressure countries to ignore their own constitutional rejection of life imprisonment, and on pain of having aid budgets and other forms of interstate cooperation threatened, to grant extradition without a condition that a life sentence may not be imposed. However, the ambiguity of the life sentence plays a part too. While a condition that the death penalty must not be imposed is usually honoured, in the case of the life sentence, argument about what 'life' really means allows the issue of principle to be fudged.

In India, Life Sentences Are Assumed to Be for Life

Ipshita Sengupta

Ipshita Sengupta is a human rights researcher based in New Delhi. In this viewpoint, she notes that the human rights implications of life imprisonment are often overshadowed by the death penalty debate. However, she does point out that international norms frown upon life imprisonment without parole. A life sentence in India is particularly harsh, Sengupta explains, because of the overcrowding and ill-treatment of prisoners. In India, the Supreme Court has declared that life imprisonment is assumed to mean a prisoner will serve out the rest of his or her natural life behind bars. Sengupta points out, however, that the sentence can be commuted, or reduced, by executive action.

As you read, consider the following questions:

1. According to the International Covenant on Civil and Political Rights, what must be the essential aim of the penitentiary system?
2. According to Amnesty International, how many people in India were sentenced to death in 2006 and 2007?
3. A person whose death penalty has been commuted to life imprisonment must serve at least how many years of imprisonment, according to Indian law?

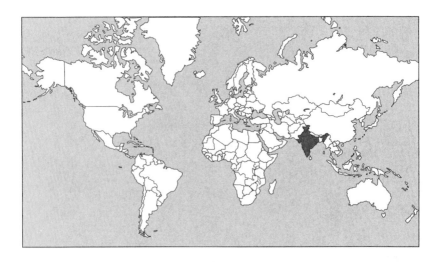

As Mohammad Afzal Guru, charged in the December 13, 2001, [terrorist] attack on the Indian Parliament, awaits a final decision on his clemency petition [to set aside his execution] pending before the president and Indian civil society deliberates on the abolition of death penalty, no attention is paid to the human rights implications of the alternative to the death penalty: life imprisonment.

International Standards for Life Imprisonment

In countries where death penalty has been abolished, life imprisonment is the maximum punishment for committing the most horrific of crimes. In most jurisdictions, however, life imprisonment does not necessarily imply a whole life in prison and lifers may be released after serving a substantial portion of their sentence, based on several mitigating factors. However, in a country like India, where death penalty is still in use, it's assumed that being a lesser punishment, life imprisonment is less retributive and more reformative in nature.

When it comes to life imprisonment, there are no set, fully developed international standards. But international human rights law allows the imposition of life sentences only in the most serious crimes and prohibits the use of life imprisonment without parole (LWOP).

The International Covenant on Civil and Political Rights (ICCPR), which came into force in 1976 and was signed and ratified by 161 countries, including India, says that the "penitentiary system shall comprise treatment of prisoners, the essential aim of which shall be their reformation and social rehabilitation". As the nongovernmental organisation Penal Reform International noted in 2007, the purpose of reformative punishment will not be served if a convict lives his or her whole life in detention without being released on parole. . . .

"When it comes to life imprisonment, there are no set, fully developed international standards. But international human rights law . . . prohibits the use of life imprisonment without parole (LWOP)."

Article 37 of the United Nations Convention on the Rights of the Child (CRC) prohibits the use of capital punishment and LWOP for offenders below the age of 18 years. The Rome Statute of the International Criminal Court provides that the maximum sentence of life imprisonment imposed on criminals convicted of grave crimes such as war crimes, crimes against humanity and genocide should be reviewed after 25 years. Although India is party to the CRC, she is opposed to the idea of an International Criminal Court and thus, is not party to the Rome Statute.

The United Nations Standard Minimum Rules for the Treatment of Prisoners lays down good practice norms for the treatment of prisoners, which are to be adhered to by prison authorities and institutions.

Life Imprisonment Is Undesirable

India continues to use the death penalty, supposedly in the 'rarest of rare' cases. Amnesty International (AI) reports that nine offences under the Indian Penal Code (IPC) and 14 other local or special laws provide for the death penalty in India. Although official figures indicate that 273 persons had been given the death sentence as of 31 December 2005, AI states that 140 persons were sentenced to death in 2006 and 2007, along with 44 others whose mercy petitions are being considered by the president of India. India has also voted against a UN General Assembly resolution calling for "a moratorium on executions with a view to abolishing the death penalty", stating that it goes against the country's statutory law.

"The lack of medical facilities and understaffing in prisons further aggravate the misery of prisoners in India. In such a situation, life imprisonment without release or parole is unhealthy and undesirable."

Given India's unwillingness to abolish the death penalty, it's interesting to study the country's position in relation to life sentences. Life imprisonment, without the possibility of release, leads to indefinite detention in prisons, and is known to cause physical, emotional and psychological distress. Prisoners could suffer from ill health, social isolation, loss of personal responsibility and identity crisis, and may even be driven to suicide. A 2007 report on Indian prisons by the Bureau of Police Research and Development, Ministry of Home Affairs, reveals that most Indian prisons are overcrowded, with inmates living in unsanitary and unhygienic conditions in small cells, without proper light, ventilation or privacy. The report notes that Indian prisons house a total of 358,368 inmates though their sanctioned strength is 246,497.

Added to this is the ill-treatment of prisoners by prison authorities, often sanctioned by outdated legislation such as the Prisons Act, 1894, and state prison manuals. For example, the 1894 act allows the imposition of corporal punishment (whipping) or solitary confinement for a limited period by

Decades of Imprisonment Without Trial in India

Machang Lalung, aged 77, was released from incarceration last month in the northeast Indian state of Assam after spending more than half a century behind bars awaiting trial.

Lalung had been arrested at his home village of Silsang in 1951 . . . for "causing grievous harm." According to civil rights groups who have investigated Lalung's case, there was no substantive evidence to support the charge against him. In any event, those found guilty of this offence typically receive sentences of no more than 10 years' imprisonment.

Less than a year after he was taken into custody, Lalung was transferred to a psychiatric hospital in the Assamese town of Tezpur. Sixteen years later, in 1967, doctors confirmed that he was "fully fit" to be released, but instead he was transferred to Guwahati Central Jail, where he was imprisoned until this summer.

"It seems the police just forgot about him thereafter," Assamese human rights activist Sanjay Borbora told the BBC. . . . As a result of the [National Human Rights] Commission's intervention and other protests, Lalung's case was finally heard and he was released after paying a token bond of one Indian rupee.

Parwini Zora, "Fifty-Four Years in Jail Without Trial: The Plight of Prison Inmates in India," CounterCurrents.org, August 26, 2005.

prison authorities for offences such as "feigning illness" or "contumaciously refusing to work". The lack of medical facilities and understaffing in prisons further aggravate the misery of prisoners in India. In such a situation, life imprisonment without release or parole is unhealthy and undesirable.

Life Sentences Are for the Whole of Life

In *Gopal Vinayak Godse vs. The Union of India*, the Supreme Court of India held that life imprisonment "must prima facie be treated as . . . imprisonment for the whole of the remaining period of the convicted person's natural life". More recently, in *Mohd. Munna vs. Union of India and Others*, the apex court held that "imprisonment for life is not equivalent to imprisonment for fourteen years or for twenty years". However, the Indian Constitution and criminal laws provide for grant of pardon and commutation of sentences [changing a sentence to a less severe one] by the president of India, governors and the executive.

"Despite the proclamation by the Indian Supreme Court that life imprisonment is for life, the power of pardon or sentence remission may be exercised to ensure early release."

Articles 72 and 161 of the Indian Constitution give the president of India and governors of states the power to grant pardon, suspension, remission or commutation of sentences in certain cases. Sections 54 and 55 of the Indian Penal Code (IPC) confer on the appropriate government—central or state governments—the power to commute sentence of death or life imprisonment. Section 432 of the Code of Criminal Procedure (CrPC) also gives the power to remit or suspend sentences, with or without conditions, to the appropriate government. Section 433 of the CrPC empowers the appropriate government to commute a life sentence for a term up to 14 years or a fine, without the consent of the person so convicted.

However, certain restrictions have been placed on the power of remission under Section 433A of the CrPC. According to this section, a person serving a life sentence for an offence for which death sentence is also a punishment or where a death sentence has been commuted to a life sentence cannot be released before serving at least 14 years of imprisonment.

The Executive May Reduce Life Sentences

The power of remission or commutation was justified in a plethora of court decisions on the ground that "public welfare will be better served by inflicting less than what the judgment fixed". While the sentencing power lies with the judiciary, the power to commute such sentences is largely executive in nature. In *Kehar Singh [and Anr.] vs. Union of India*, the Supreme Court clarified that the constitutional power of grant of pardon or the executive power of remission does not conflict with the judicial power of passing a judgment. The effect of the executive power of remission is to "remove the stigma of guilt from the accused or to remit the sentence imposed on him". . . .

A look at the jail manuals and rules in different Indian states shows that lifers are not entitled to automatic release after serving 20 years of the life sentence. However, they do earn the right to have their case for remission put forth before the state government by the prison authorities. . . .

Despite the proclamation by the Indian Supreme Court that life imprisonment is for life, the power of pardon or sentence remission may be exercised to ensure early release. As Justice Laurie Ackermann of the South African Constitutional Court observed in the case of *S vs. Dodo*, "To attempt to justify any period of penal incarceration, let alone imprisonment for life . . . without inquiring into the proportionality between the offence and the period of imprisonment, is to ignore, if not to deny, that which lies at the very heart of dignity. Human beings are not commodities to which a price can be attached; they are creatures with inherent and infinite worth; they ought to be treated as ends in themselves, never merely as means to an end."

In Singapore, Juveniles Can Be Detained Indefinitely

Chong Chee Kin and Teh Joo Lin

Chong Chee Kin is a news editor and Teh Joo Lin is a crime reporter, both at the Straits Times. *In this viewpoint, they report that in Singapore, juveniles who commit capital crimes cannot be sentenced to death. Instead they are detained "at the president's pleasure," which means they remain in jail until the executive decides to release them. Critics argue that uncertainty makes these sentences excessively harsh and deprives juvenile prisoners of hope. They argue that sentencing options should be reviewed, the authors report, giving judges more discretion to provide fixed terms of imprisonment in juvenile cases.*

As you read, consider the following questions:

1. In Singapore, criminals younger than what age may not receive the death penalty?

2. According to a December 2001 report, what was the longest detention served by a juvenile in Singapore at that time?

3. Besides being imprisoned at the president's pleasure, what act in Singapore provides another sentencing option for juvenile offenders?

Chong Chee Kin and Teh Joo Lin, "Just Punishment or Too Harsh?" *The Straits Times*, May 24, 2008. Copyright © 2008 Singapore Press Holdings Ltd. Reproduced by permission.

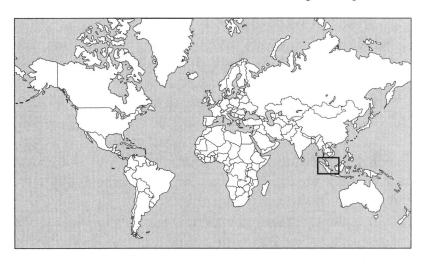

In prison right now, there are seven youths with no inkling of when they would be released. They were aged below 18 when they committed their crimes.

That is what it means to be detained at the President's pleasure: You enter the slammer not knowing when you will get out. Young people who commit capital crimes that would have sent them straight to the gallows had they been older can be sentenced to such a term. It is provided for by Singapore's Criminal Procedure Code (CPC), which states that criminals below 18 cannot receive the death penalty.

Last month, Muhammad Nasir Abdul Aziz was sentenced thus after being convicted of killing his lover's husband. He was 16 when he committed the crime last July.

"That is what it means to be detained at the President's pleasure: You enter the slammer not knowing when you will get out."

A prisons spokesman confirms there are seven such detainees now. No names were revealed but reports since 1993 indicate that youths detained in the past included three boys who fatally attacked a 15-year-old boy with wooden poles, a

14-year-old boy who stabbed a woman in the heart, as well as a teen couple found with 19.7kg of opium. Two of the nine reported cases in the past were girls who were detained at the President's pleasure.

Their prison regime is not very different from that of the other inmates, a prisons spokesman said. 'Depending on their conduct and behaviour, they can also work in workshops within the institution or be placed in vocational and educational programmes. They are also given opportunities for family contact through regular visits.'

The prisons authorities have not disclosed the shortest and longest terms served by youths. The last time they revealed such details was in a December 2001 report. Between 1969 and 2001, 10 young prisoners were granted clemency. The shortest detention was for seven years, the longest, 26. In the same report, the authorities said 14 youths were detained at the President's pleasure at the time.

In response to a query from the *Straits Times*, a Ministry of Home Affairs spokesman said such cases are reviewed annually.

'The person's conduct and progress are monitored and reviewed annually. When the offender is found suitable for release, a recommendation will be made to the President, who may then direct the release of the offender,' the spokesman said.

When a youth is released depends on his behaviour and how well he responds to rehabilitation, the prisons spokesman said, adding that there are 'established processes and guidelines' for the review. Any inmate can also petition the President for clemency.

The indefinite period of incarceration has prompted some in the legal fraternity to ask if the punishment is too heavy.

The provision in the CPC that allows for such detention was inherited from colonial times. In Britain, youths below 18 who commit murder are sentenced to detention at Her Majesty's pleasure.

In the U.S., Children Are Tried and Imprisoned as Adults

In forty-two states and under federal law, the commission of a serious crime by children under eighteen—indeed in some states children as young as ten—transforms them instantly into adults for criminal justice purposes. Children who are too young to buy cigarettes legally, boys who may not have started to get facial hair, kids who still have stuffed animals on their beds, are tried as adults, and if convicted, receive adult prison sentences, including life without parole (LWOP). . . .

Human Rights Watch and Amnesty International have discovered that there are currently at least 2,225 people incarcerated in the United States who have been sentenced to spend the rest of their lives in prison for crimes they committed as children. . . .

The public may believe that children who receive life without parole sentences are "super-predators" with long records of vicious crimes. In fact, an estimated 59 percent received the sentence for their first-ever criminal conviction. Sixteen percent were between thirteen and fifteen years old at the time they committed their crimes. While the vast majority were convicted of murder, an estimated 26 percent were convicted of felony murder in which the teen participated in a robbery or burglary during which a co-participant committed murder, without the knowledge or intent of the teen.

Human Rights Watch and Amnesty International,
The Rest of their Lives, *October 11, 2005, www.hrw.org*

Minimum jail terms—meted out at the judge's discretion—are set for each offender. These must be serve before a parole board can consider releasing them.

In Singapore's case, no minimum or maximum incarceration period needs to be specified, as National University of Singapore law don Chan Wing Cheong noted. But he pointed out there is another sentencing option under the Children and Young Persons Act (CYPA) for those who commit heinous crimes. Under this law, a youth who commits murder can get a definite sentence of imprisonment.

"'From the inmate's point of view, not knowing exactly when he could be released is a form of punishment in itself.'"

Associate Professor Chan feels that a review is necessary in view of what he sees as a 'conflict between sentencing options'. He even suggests abolishing detention at the President's pleasure.

In a letter to the *Straits Times* Forum Page last month, he wrote: 'A defined term of imprisonment offers more hope to young persons and therefore assists in rehabilitation.'

Four years ago, then-state prosecutor Paul Quan wrote a paper on a 15-year-old student jailed for killing a woman at the urging of her ex-husband.

Mr Quan, now a magistrate, argued that jailing the boy for an indefinite period was a severe penalty in sharp contrast to the CYPA, which allows a judge to exercise discretion in deciding an appropriate sentence.

Such discretion, he argued, was potentially appropriate in view of the 'strongly worded' concessions the trial judge made about the boy's nature. Mr Quan's article, written in his personal capacity, was published in the *Singapore Academy of Law Journal*.

Veteran criminal lawyer Subhas Anandan agrees that sentencing options should be reviewed. And the time to do it would be now, since the CPC is being reviewed this year.

Mr Subhas, president of the Association of Criminal Lawyers of Singapore, said: 'From the inmate's point of view, not knowing exactly when he could be released is a form of punishment in itself.'

Dr Teo Ho Pin, chairman of the Government Parliamentary Committee for Law and Home Affairs, however, thinks indefinite detention for youths should stay.

It sends out a 'strong deterrent message' to the young, he said. If they commit severe crimes, they should not expect to escape harsh penalties.

'This has to sink in well, rather than the notion that they will be protected. They are not 11 or 12 years old. They should know what they are doing,' he said.

Honduran Juveniles Must Not Be Sentenced to Adult Jails

Melissa Ewer

In 2007, Melissa Ewer was a staff attorney for the Catholic Charities Violence Against Women Act (VAWA) Immigration Project in Albuquerque, New Mexico. According to Ewer in the following excerpt, Honduras has a growing number of street children (an estimated eight thousand in 2001). About 40 percent of these children engage in prostitution, and about 30 percent of the street children in two major Honduran cities are HIV positive. Because juvenile detention centers are lacking, when street children are detained, they are often kept in adult prisons, where they are abused. Much of this abuse comes from prison security force personnel, who sometimes torture and abuse inmates including street children. Corruption within security forces and the consequent inability to control crime has led to an increase in vigilante justice, and this has resulted in the deaths of some street children. Laws against torture and arbitrary detention exist, but those in the Honduran legal system lack the will and/or the ability to defend the street children from these abuses.

As you read, consider the following questions:

1. How many times is Casa Alianza mentioned? What does it do?

Melissa Ewer, "Part I: Background Information: Honduras," *From the Streets to the States: Asylum Claims from Guatemalan and Honduran Street Children*, Washington, D.C.: American Immigration Law Foundation, 2001. Copyright © 2001 American Immigration Law Foundation, (www.ailf.org). Reproduced by permission.

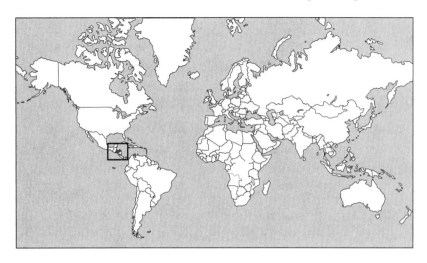

2. What is the significance of Hurricane Mitch?

3. What does the term "social cleansing" refer to?

General Economic and Human Rights Conditions. Honduras is one of the most economically disadvantaged countries in the Western Hemisphere, with an economy primarily dependent on coffee and bananas. The country has a poorly developed infrastructure and is extremely dependent on foreign aid. Honduras has been historically dependent on the United States in particular. Its annual per capita income is approximately $800 and about two-thirds of the country's households live in poverty.

In 1982, Honduras elected Roberto Suazo Córdova, the country's first civilian president after a decade of military rule. Since the late 1960s, armed forces have evolved as a principal political force, either by governing directly, influencing general policy, or controlling national security affairs. The country's National Police was just transferred to civilian control in 1997 yet members of the police continued to commit human rights abuses in 1999. Also, throughout the 1980s, Honduras's involvement in Central American politics deepened as the country expanded military ties with the United States through in-creased levels of military aid, modification and construction of airfields, the establishment of a regional training center, and a series of large military exercises. As conflicts in the neighboring countries of El Salvador and Nicaragua intensi-fied, Honduras's strategic location served as both a haven for refugees and a device for US intervention in Cold War poli-tics.

More recently, in 1998, Hurricane Mitch devastated Hon-duras, causing deaths, homelessness for hundreds of thou-sands and over three billion dollars worth of damage to the country's infrastructure, and a 10% increase in the number of street children in the capital city of Tegucigalpa. The president also ordered the temporary suspension of certain civil liberties as a result of the hurricane. The US State Department reports that

> [i]nternational humanitarian assistance saved many lives and met basic needs, but substantial additional foreign aid is needed to help rebuild infrastructure and productive eco-nomic capacity. The economic growth rate declined in 1999, and the budget deficit and unemployment both rose signifi-cantly.

Also active in Honduras, Casa Alianza has observed that the country is out of step with the rest of Central America in efforts to reduce the age of criminal responsibility for chil-dren. Honduras had been trying to change the age of criminal responsibility from 18 years old to 14 years old, even though minors do NOT commit 54.5% of the crimes in the country and do NOT commit 99.8% of homicides.

Like Guatemala, Honduras has signed the UN Convention on the Rights of the Child (CRC). The convention was signed on May 31, 1990, and entered into force a few months later on September 9, 1990. As noted by UNICEF, the CRC "states frequently that states need to identify the most vulnerable and disadvantaged children within their borders and take affirmative action to ensure that the rights of these children are realized and protected." The guiding principles include non-discrimination, best interests of the child, maximum survival and development and participation of children. Keeping in mind these principles and obligations imposed on Honduras by the CRC, the sections of this paper that follow illustrate Honduras's treatment of street children, the persistence of police brutality and the ineffectiveness of the country's judicial system.

"Similar to the situation in Guatemala, more than 75% of Honduran street children found their way to the streets because of severe family problems; 30% simply were abandoned."

Street Children. As in Guatemala, street children in Honduras face bleak living conditions. According to Casa Alianza, the street children of Honduras are particularly "very dirty, generally do not wear shoes[,] . . . have leftovers of glue in their bodies, show malnutrition [and] evidence of skin diseases, . . . [have] problems with their respiratory system and suffer venereal diseases." The US State Department has noted that the Honduran government has been unable to prevent the abuse of street children and human rights groups have repeatedly implicated members of the security forces in a number of killings of street children. Also, due to a general lack of juvenile detention centers, street children in detention were often housed in adult prisons where they were routinely abused.

The presence of street children in Honduras is becoming more widespread. According to Casa Alianza, one new child in the capital city of Tegucigalpa is forced to go to the streets every day. The Honduran government recently raised its estimate of the number of street children to 8,000, only half of whom have shelter on any given day. The plight of these children looks strikingly similar to that of Guatemalan street children. Many street children have been molested sexually and about 40% regularly engage in prostitution. Additionally, approximately 30% of street children in Tegucigalpa and San Pedro Sula, the principal urban centers in Honduras, were HIV positive. Frequent inhalant use by children is also a problem: At least 40% of Honduran street children are addicted to sniffing glue. Similar to the situation in Guatemala, more than 75% of Honduran street children found their way to the streets because of severe family problems; 30% simply were abandoned.

To exacerbate the situation, the number of children on the street increased substantially as a result of Hurricane Mitch. It was predicted that the population of street children in Honduras would double in the three months following the wrath of Hurricane Mitch. Indeed, Casa Alianza's own crisis centre was left unusable by the natural disaster. As in Guatemala, both the Honduran police ("death squads") and members of the general population who participated in vigilante groups engaged in violence against street children. The State Department notes that "human rights groups implicated out-of-uniform security force personnel, vigilantes, and business leaders in some juvenile deaths." As will be illustrated in the following section, the prevalence of police brutality presents a crisis for street children in Honduras.

Police Brutality and the Lack of an Effective Judicial System. Control of the National Police in Honduras was only recently transferred to civilians in 1997 and although reports of human rights abuses have declined since the police were separated from the military forces, members of the police continue to commit abuses. Reports from 1999 indicate that security force personnel committed acts of torture and otherwise abused detainees and others, including street children. Indeed, in June of 1999, the attorney general of Honduras "acknowl-

Central American Prison Statistics

Country	Total Prison Population	Incarceration Rate per 100,000	Year of Data
Belize	1,359	487	2006
Costa Rica	7,782	181	2006
El Salvador	12,176	174	2005
Guatemala	7,227	57	2005
Honduras	11,589	161	2005
Mexico	214,450	196	2006
Nicaragua	5,610	98	2005
Panama	11,649	364	2006

TAKEN FROM: Roy Walmsley, *World Population Prison List*, 7th ed., International Centre for Prison Studies, 2006. www.kcl.ac.uk.

edged that security force personnel continue to commit acts of torture, due in part to poor training and lack of knowledge regarding human rights obligations." Additionally, human rights organizations have alleged that current and former members of the security forces, acting as vigilante "security squadrons," committed extra-judicial killings during recent years. According to Andrés Pavón, president of the nongovernmental Committee for the Defense of Human Rights in Honduras, death squads have ties to the Honduran government and are financed by businesses "obsessed with eliminating alleged criminals."

Similar to circumstances in Guatemala, dramatic increases in violent crime fueled the continued growth in the number of private, often unlicensed, guard services, and of volunteer groups who patrolled their neighborhoods or municipalities to deter crime. As the US State Department notes, "The continued proliferation of private security forces made it more difficult to differentiate among homicides that may have been perpetrated by government security personnel, private vigilantes, or common criminals." Widespread frustration at the inability of the security forces to prevent and control crime, along with an accurate perception that corrupt security personnel were complicit in the high crime rate, led to considerable public support for vigilante justice. During the past few years, vigilante justice led to killings of street children and criminals. In October 1999, the US State Department asserts, a vigilante group in Cortés department reportedly beat and killed a young man with no known criminal connections. In 1998, with congressional support, the president deployed 600 army troops in the country's four major cities to assist the National Police in curtailing rising street crime, despite the official separation of the military from the police forces. Once again in March 1999, President [Carlos Roberto] Flores ordered the military to reinforce the National Police and conduct joint patrols throughout Honduras, in an effort to reduce crime during the Easter holiday season.

As can be surmised from the preceding paragraphs, the social cleansing trend exists in Honduras just as it does in Guatemala. Between 100 and 150 youths associated with criminal gangs were killed execution-style in 1999. In such cases, renegade elements of the security forces, or civilian (including vigilante) groups working with such elements, allegedly used unjustifiable deadly force against supposed habitual criminals. The Honduran government did not effectively act to try, convict, or punish anyone for these offenses.

Although there are laws against torture, arbitrary detention and arbitrary arrest, authorities occasionally do not observe these legal requirements in practice. One striking example of Honduran governmental authorities acting outside the boundaries of law occurred on January 21, 2000, in the community of San Antonio, municipality of San Jerónimo, Comayagua. On that date, a police officer shot and killed at point blank range a handcuffed and unarmed 17-year-old Edy Nahum Donaire Ortega who had escaped illegal detention at a police station. International law allows for the use of mortal force by a police officer only when the officer's life is in imminent danger. As Bruce Harris of Casa Alianza points out, "shooting a minor at point blank range is obviously a violation of these norms." Unfortunately, as will be demonstrated, Honduras is not equipped with a legal system that is both willing and able to bring to justice those who commit crimes against street children.

"Between 100 and 150 youths associated with criminal gangs were killed execution-style in 1999."

Although the Honduran government respects constitutional provisions in principle, implementation has been weak and uneven in practice. As in Guatemala, the judiciary in Honduras is independent, but often ineffective and subject to outside influence. Members of the economic and official elite in Honduras enjoy a great deal of impunity, aggravated by a weak, underfunded and sometimes corrupt judicial system. This contributes to the country's problems respecting human rights. Although civilian courts increasingly considered allegations of human rights violations or common crimes perpetrated by armed forces personnel and some cases went to trial, there were relatively few convictions. In fact, amnesty is often granted to military officials. Notwithstanding, the attorney general and human rights groups have noted a decrease in reported human rights abuses over the past 2 years. To be sure, the US State Department notes,

> The Office of Professional Responsibility (OPR) within the National Police investigates allegations of torture and abuse and can recommend sanctions against police agents found guilty of such mistreatment. However, neither the police commander nor the OPR is empowered to punish wrongdoers; only the immediate superior of the accused agent has the authority to do so. The Public Ministry and human

rights groups criticized the OPR for being unresponsive to their requests for impartial investigations of police officers accused of abuses. In 1996 the Public Ministry created the office of Human Rights Inspector within the DGIC [Departamento General de Investigación Criminal/General Criminal Investigation Department] to monitor the behavior of its agents; the inspector reports to the head of the human rights section of the Public Ministry and to the attorney general. Both the DGIC and the preventive police dismissed or suspended dozens of agents and officials for abuse of authority.

However, elements of the armed forces withheld their cooperation from official efforts to locate military officers sought after in connection with alleged human rights abuses dating back to the 1980s. In addition, the judiciary and Public Ministry suffer from insufficient funding and low wages, making law enforcement officials vulnerable to bribery and powerful special interests. As in previous years, in 1999, the judicial system continued to deny swift and impartial justice to prisoners awaiting trial. Also, although positive steps were taken to investigate human rights abuses, abuse of power, fraud and diversion of public funds by former ranking government officials and by military officers, none of the accused were tried or convicted. Indeed, cases are often dismissed for lack of evidence.

The Honduran Constitution bans discrimination on the basis of class, but in fact, the political, military and social elites generally enjoyed impunity before the legal system. The Constitution also prohibits torture and provides for the right to a fair trial and an independent judiciary, but reality does not conform to these provisions either. As a result, the effects of the combination of police brutality and an ineffective judicial system override these beneficial intentions of the Constitution. . . .

Canadians Support Mandatory Sentencing with Some Judicial Discretion

Julian V. Roberts, Nicole Crutcher, and Paul Verbrugge

Julian V. Roberts is a professor of criminology at the University of Ottawa; Nicole Crutcher and Paul Verbrugge are both scholars and writers. In the following viewpoint, the authors argue that while mandatory sentencing is politically popular, it is important to allow for judicial discretion—allow judges the power to moderate sentences in exceptional circumstances. Mandatory sentencing laws in Canada do not allow judges that power. The authors argue that, based on polling, Canadians actually support allowing judges some discretion in sentencing.

As you read, consider the following questions:

1. Why did the Supreme Court of Canada rule that the seven-year minimum sentence of imprisonment for drug trafficking was unconstitutional?

2. According to the authors, what percentage of Canadians surveyed could not cite any offenses carrying a mandatory minimum sentence?

Julian V. Roberts, Nicole Crutcher, and Paul Verbrugge, "Public Attitudes to Sentencing in Canada: Exploring Recent Findings," *Canadian Journal of Criminology and Criminal Justice*, vol. 49, no. 1, January 2007, pp. 75–108. Copyright © University of Toronto Press 2007. Reprinted by permission of University of Toronto Press Incorporated www.utpjournals.com, www.ccja-acjp.cca/en/.

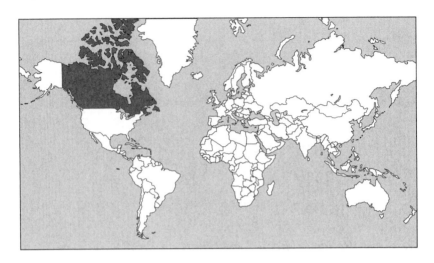

3. According to the authors, what percentage of Canadians surveyed agreed with allowing judicial discretion in the context of direction from Parliament as to when a sentence below the mandatory minimum could be imposed?

Most Western nations have enacted mandatory sentencing legislation in recent years [minimum sentences for certain crimes established by law]. These laws usually focus on serious, violent and repeat offenders. The mandatory sentences of imprisonment in some jurisdictions are particularly severe. For example, in South Africa, the Criminal Law Amendment Act 105 of 1997 created long mandatory sentences of imprisonment for a range of offences, particularly when the offender has previous convictions. An offender convicted of robbery for the third or subsequent occasion must be sentenced to at least 25 years in prison. Mandatory sentencing laws have usually been introduced to address escalating crime rates (or perceptions of rising crime rates) and to respond to public pressure to make the sentencing process harsher.

Mandatory Sentencing Is Politically Popular

For many politicians, mandatory sentences represent a convenient, expeditious, and popular response to a specific crime problem. Since polls repeatedly show that the public believes sentencing to be excessively lenient, any reform that promises greater severity is perceived to be consistent with public opinion. For example, an Australian prime minister stated several years ago that he was "not surprised at the overwhelming support that Australians have shown for the introduction of mandatory sentencing laws." He was referring, however, not to a scientific survey using a representative sample but simply to a tabloid newspaper initiative in which interested readers had been asked to express their opinions on the issue. Politicians' interpretation of public opinion in this area may be erroneous; public support for mandatory sentencing may be not as strong as many suppose. Contrary evidence can be found in a poll conducted in the United States in 1999, which found that more than half of the sample stated that they would be more likely to vote for a politician who advocated increasing judicial discretion—the antithesis to mandatory sentencing.

The fatal shooting in Toronto on Boxing Day 2005 of teenager Jane Creba shocked Canadians and resulted in calls for more and more severe mandatory sentences of imprisonment for firearms offences. The fact that this crime took place during the middle of a federal election gave additional impetus to the movement to amend the existing mandatory sentence provisions of the Criminal Code. . . . Once elected, the new federal government moved swiftly to introduce mandatory sentencing legislation.

Bill C-10 was introduced on 4 May 2006 for the purpose of amending the Criminal Code with respect to sentencing for firearms offences. The legislation calls for a number of amendments, including increasing the four-year minimum for certain firearms offences to five years for first-time offenders. The legislation also provides for escalating minimum penalties for repeat offenders. For example, for a second conviction of a specified firearms offence (e.g., robbery with firearm), the minimum sentence would be seven years imprisonment; if there is a third conviction, the minimum sentence would rise to 10 years. There are also several firearms offences that currently carry a one-year minimum sentence, which, if the legislation is passed, will increase to three years for a first conviction and five years for any subsequent convictions. The legislation also aims to create two new offences: breaking and entering with intent to steal a firearm and robbery with intent to steal a firearm. A conviction for either of these two offences would result in a three-year minimum sentence for a first conviction and a five-year minimum sentence for any subsequent convictions. . . .

Most Nations Allow Judicial Discretion

Mandating a long prison sentence for a specific crime, regardless of the individual circumstances of the offence or the offender, has the potential to create injustices. There will always be cases that are less serious than the typical crime. For this reason, mandatory sentencing legislation in most countries permits a limited degree of judicial discretion [judges can reduce sentences]. Courts are empowered to impose a less severe sentence of imprisonment—or even a non-custodial disposition [a sentence other than imprisonment]—in the event that exceptional circumstances exist to justify a lesser sentence. . . .

Even in South Africa, the nation with some of the most severe mandatory sentences outside the United States and arguably the worst crime problem, judges are able to exercise some judicial discretion to circumvent the mandatory minimum sentence. . . .

The experience in South Africa suggests that exceptional circumstances are often invoked by courts to circumvent the mandatory sentence.

"Mandatory sentencing legislation in most countries permits a limited degree of judicial discretion."

In Canada, There Is No Judicial Discretion

One of the features of Canadian mandatory minima that sets them apart from mandatory sentences elsewhere is the absence of any provision for judicial discretion. It is significant that none of the proposals for additional mandatory sentences made during the election—nor the government's amendments to existing mandatories—includes any "judicial discretion" clause. With respect to the firearms mandatory minima introduced in 1995, courts must impose a term of at least four years if the offender has been convicted of one of the 10 enumerated offences using a firearm. . . . The minimum sentence must be imposed regardless of the individual circumstances of the case or whether the interests of justice would be best achieved with a lesser sentence.

Permitting courts some flexibility with mandatory minimum sentencing regimes is important particularly if the mandatory sentence is very long. It is inevitable that circumstances will arise that sometimes justify the imposition of a lesser sentence. "Judicial discretion" clauses of this nature are often overlooked; when crafting and approving mandatory-sentencing statutes, legislators usually have in mind the most serious cases of any particular offence. When the mandatory sentence is applied, however, judges are sometimes confronted with crimes committed in exceptional circumstances that are far less serious than those envisaged by the legislature and do not correspond to the profile targeted by the drafters of the legislation. Some politicians appear to respond to a category of offending—serious gun crime—and have no experience with the wide diversity of offences and offenders that appear for sentencing in criminal courts across the country. This is why it makes little sense for legislators to intervene with such inflexible and blunt sentencing tools as a statutory mandatory minimum at this level in the sentencing process.

A good example of this phenomenon can be found in the history of sentencing in Canada. It will be recalled that the Supreme Court of Canada struck down the seven-year minimum sentence of imprisonment for drug trafficking in *R. v. Smith* (1987). This sentence was originally legislated to ensure that large-scale traffickers received a severe penalty and to thereby promote general deterrence. In practice, most of the offenders affected by this mandatory sentence were drug couriers, often young people on vacation in the Caribbean. The penal net had caught the wrong fish. This failure on the part of the legislation to address the problem for which the mandatory penalty was conceived was one of the reasons why the Court ruled that the mandatory sentence was unconstitutional, as it violated s. 12 of the Canadian Charter of Rights and Freedoms, which prohibits cruel and unusual punishment. . . .

"Judges are sometimes confronted with crimes committed in exceptional circumstances that are far less serious than those envisaged by the legislature and do not correspond to the profile targeted by the drafters of the legislation."

Public Knowledge of Mandatory Minimum Sentences

Before exploring public attitudes toward mandatory sentencing, we note the findings from a question that tested public knowledge of the mandatory minima currently set out in the Criminal Code.

The principal objectives of a mandatory sentence of imprisonment are to promote the deterrent power of the criminal law and to express denunciation of the offence for which the sentence is imposed. However, potential offenders will be deterred only if they are aware of the sentences, and denunciation will be possible only if the community knows about the denunciatory sentence. The Supreme Court of Canada noted as much in *R. v. Morrisey*, a leading mandatory sentence case wherein the Court observed that the minimum sentence concerned "serves the principle of denunciation." An important research question, therefore, is whether people are aware of the existence and severity of the current mandatory penalties. Absent a database of potential offenders, researchers generally use public knowledge as an indication of the extent to which these penalties are known.

Prior to being asked the questions about mandatory sentencing, participants were provided with the following definition:

A mandatory minimum sentence would be a jail sentence where the minimum length of time for a conviction of a specific crime has been set by Parliament and a judge may not go below the minimum sentence.

The open-ended knowledge question asked people to state which offences, aside from murder, currently carry a mandatory minimum sentence in Canada. The most common offence cited was "drunk driving," but even this well-known crime was identified by fewer than one respondent in five (19%). Almost half (43%) of the respondents could not cite any offences carrying a mandatory minimum sentence, despite there being 31 offences with such a penalty at the time the survey was conducted. The general lack of awareness of the mandatory minimum sentencing regime was evident in the fact that no other offence was cited by more than 7% of the sample. Seven percent identified assault, 6% firearms offences, and 5% violent offences. These responses may well reflect guesswork rather than knowledge on the part of respondents, and they undermine arguments used to promote mandatory

Public Attitudes Towards Various Sentencing Purposes, Canada, 2005

% respondents identifying objective as

Sentencing Purpose	The Single Most Important Purpose (%)	Very Important (%)	Somewhat Important (%)	Not Very Important (%)	Not At All Important (%)
Make offenders acknowledge and take responsibility for crime	27	84	14	2	0
Make offenders repair the harm caused by offence	13	66	27	4	1
Individual deterrence	12	63	26	7	3
Satisfying the victim that "justice was done"	9	59	32	7	2

continued

Public Attitudes Towards Various Sentencing Purposes, Canada, 2005 [CONTINUED]

% respondents identifying objective as

Sentencing Purpose	The Single Most Important Purpose (%)	Very Important (%)	Somewhat Important (%)	Not Very Important (%)	Not At All Important (%)
General deterrence	9	53	32	10	5
Rehabilitation	11	51	38	7	2
Incapacitation	9	40	41	11	3
Denunciation of the crime	3	39	41	13	4

TAKEN FROM: Julian V. Roberts, Nicole Crutcher and Paul Verbrugge, "Public Attitudes to Sentencing in Canada: Exploring Recent Findings," *Canadian Journal of Criminology and Criminal Justice*, vol. 49, no. 1, January 2007, pp. 75–108.

minimum sentences. If Canadians do not know they exist—
even in the case of driving while impaired, which has received
extensive media coverage—how can these sentences be effective in preventing or denouncing crime?

---

*"Potential offenders will be deterred only if they are
aware of the sentences, and denuciation will be possible
only if the community knows about the denunciatory
sentence."*

These results are not unique to this survey; they are consistent with the findings from surveys conducted in 1985. The
CSC [Canadian Sentencing Commission] found that only
16% of the polled public correctly identified impaired driving
as an offence carrying a mandatory sentence of imprisonment, and this poll was conducted at a time of heightened attention to impaired driving laws. Research in other jurisdictions has found the same low levels of public awareness. Less
than one-quarter of the respondents to the 1998 British Crime
Survey were aware of the mandatory minimum penalty for offenders convicted of a third or subsequent burglary. In this respect, mandatory sentences are no different from other statutory elements of the sentencing process: Their existence
escapes the attention of the general public. These findings call
into question any potential general deterrent or denunciatory
effects of mandatory sentences of custody. . . .

Public Attitudes Towards
Mandatory Sentencing

There are obvious limitations associated with questions that
explore public attitudes on a general level. When people are
asked whether sentences are too lenient or too harsh, or
whether prisoners should be eligible for parole, they tend to
have the worst-case offence and offender in mind. As noted
earlier, general questions about sentencing and parole encour-

age people to think of the worst-case scenario: violent offenders with significant criminal histories. However, since general questions are used so frequently, one was posed in this survey for purposes of comparison.

Respondents were asked the following question, which provided some context by identifying the primary advantage or justification for mandatory sentences, as well as the primary disadvantage. . .:

> Some people say that mandatory minimum sentences are generally a bad idea because they are too inflexible and don't allow judges to consider any special circumstances. Other people say that mandatory minimum sentences are generally a good idea because they ensure that offences are properly punished. Which of these points of view is closest to your own?

Three response options were provided: "minimum sentences are a good idea," "minimum sentences are a bad idea," and "depends." (Respondents could also respond "don't know" or not respond at all.) Only 5% responded "depends," while slightly more than half the sample (58%) held the view that these sentences were a good idea and 36% held the view that they were a bad idea (1% responded "don't know"). On a general level, then, there was more support for than opposition to mandatory sentencing—although the level of support was far from overwhelming. . . .

There is considerable consistency across three jurisdictions with respect to public attitudes to mandatory sentencing. Polls in three countries conducted at different times over a 10-year period reveal almost exactly the same level of support for mandatory sentencing.

Public Justifications for Mandatory Sentences

The two principal justifications for creating a mandatory sentence of imprisonment are deterrence and denunciation. Advocates of deterrence assume that the certainty and severity of a specified custodial punishment for a targeted offence will alone reduce the incidence of that offence. The mandatory sentences of imprisonment for a second or subsequent impaired driving offence are representative of penalties justified in this way. However, mandatory minimum sentences may also be justified on the grounds of denunciation. Some crimes are so serious—so the argument runs—that only a sentence of institutional imprisonment is adequate to denounce the criminal conduct. The mandatory sentence of life imprisonment for first- and second-degree murder is the best example of a sentence justified on the basis of denunciation. Murder is regarded as such a serious offence—even in the presence of mitigating factors such as the absence of previous convictions—that no lesser sentence would constitute a punishment acceptable to the community.

Which of these two justifications—deterrence or denunciation—underlies public support for mandatory sentences? Comparative levels of support were tested by the following question the wording of which reflects findings from the latest empirical research into the effectiveness of general deterrence:

> What if you knew that research showed that for certain kinds of offences, mandatory minimum sentences did not reduce the likelihood of offenders re-offending. Would you agree or disagree with still having a mandatory minimum applied to those offences?

Fully two-thirds of the public still agreed with the existence of a mandatory sentence, suggesting that the public is interested in mandatory sentencing more for the purpose of denunciation than for the purpose of deterrence. . . .

The next question asked whether there should be mandatory sentences for all crimes, most, some, or none at all. Less than one-quarter of respondents favoured the existence of a mandatory sentence for all crimes; the option attracting the most support was "only some crimes," supported by 38%.

One-third favoured a mandatory sentence for most crimes, while 7% supported mandatory sentences for no crimes and 1% responded "don't know." The fact that most respondents rejected the application of mandatory sentencing to all crimes is the first evidence from this survey of public support for preserving judicial discretion at sentencing.

A subsequent question asked respondents to identify the specific offences for which a mandatory sentence is appropriate. The pattern of responses to this question suggests a link in the public mind between the seriousness level of an offence and the need for a mandatory sentence. Exactly half the sample cited murder, and slightly over one-third (35%) cited sexual assault. It is interesting to note that fewer than one respondent in 10 identified impaired driving and only one in 20 cited an offence involving a firearm. After sexual assault, the next most frequently cited crimes were assault and any offence involving violence (13%). . . .

"The public is interested in mandatory sentencing more for the purpose of denunciation than for the purpose of deterrence."

Canadians Support Judicial Discretion

As noted [previously], the Canadian mandatory minimum sentences allow no judicial discretion to impose a lesser sentence in the event that exceptional circumstances exist or when the interests of justice justify such an outcome. We probed public reaction to the concept of a mandatory minimum sentence that permits some limited judicial discretion using the following question:

> Do you agree or disagree that there should be some flexibility for a judge to impose less than the mandatory minimum sentence under special circumstances? Would that be strongly or somewhat?

Responses demonstrate strong public support for the concept of judicial discretion. Approximately three-quarters of the sample (74%) agreed with the idea (30% strongly agreed, and 44% somewhat agreed). Slightly less than one-quarter (24%) disagreed (10% strongly disagreed, while 10% somewhat disagreed and 2% responded "don't know").

Two additional questions approached the issue of judicial discretion in another way, and the robust nature of public support for judicial discretion clearly emerged. First, respondents were asked whether they would strongly agree, somewhat agree, somewhat disagree, or strongly disagree with allowing a court to impose a lesser sentence if the judge had to provide a written justification for a decision in which he or she goes below the mandatory minimum sentence. In response to this question, 72% agreed and 26% disagreed with the existence of judicial discretion under these conditions. The second question asked whether people agreed or disagreed with allowing a judge to impose a sentence below the mandatory minimum term if Parliament had outlined clear guidelines for the exercise of discretion in this way. In this case, 68% agreed and 30% disagreed with allowing judicial discretion in the context of direction from Parliament as to when a sentence below the minimum could be imposed.

Taken together, these three questions suggest that there is strong support among members of the Canadian public for the kind of mandatory sentence regimes found in other common law jurisdictions such as England and Wales and South Africa. The lesson from these findings is that the existing minima, as well as the more punitive proposals contained in the recent legislative proposals, are inconsistent with the views of the Canadian public.

In Britain and Germany, Innovative Sentences Increase Chances for Rehabilitation

House of Commons Home Affairs Committee

The House of Commons Home Affairs Committee is a commit-tee of Parliament in Britain that investigates government activities concerning immigration and passports, drug policy, counter-terrorism, and police. In the following viewpoint, the committee argues that prison should provide constructive work for prisoners to prepare them to find employment upon release. The committee points to several examples of good practice. First, the HMP Coldingley in Surrey, England, provides full-time work for all of its prisoners. Second, the Tegel prison in Germany makes extensive use of day release passes, so prisoners can find jobs working in the community.

As you read, consider the following questions:

1. What are the three main industrial workshops at HMP Coldingley?
2. What is the one respect in which the viewpoint argues that the Coldingley regime is open to criticism?
3. In Germany, what percentage of prisoners who are granted home leave fail to return?

House of Commons Home Affairs Committee, "Part II: The Challenge for the Future: Increasing Ex-Prisoners' Opportunity to Work," *Rehabilitation of Prisoners: First Report of Session 2004–2005*, vol. 1, January 7, 2005, pp. 54–57. Reproduced by permission.

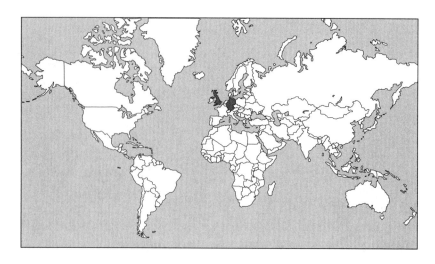

The two core aims of a prison industries strategy should be (i) provision of *constructive* work activities for the majority of the prison population when they are in prison and (ii) the employment of prisoners at the end of their sentence. In our view, the closer the work and training activities provided by prisons relate to the needs of the labour market, the greater are the chances of prisoners securing employment on release. During the course of our inquiry we have come across . . . prison work schemes which we suggest should form the basis of a modern, integrated prison work strategy. [One such] scheme is operated at HMP [Her Majesty's Prison] Coldingley [a prison in Surrey, England] and is based on the traditional prison workshop template, where the workshop is designed on the basis of a small private business. . . . We also discuss the German experience of extended use of day release, from which we think lessons can also be learnt.

The HMP Coldingley Workshop Scheme

In May 2004 we visited HMP Coldingley, a Category C industrial training prison in Surrey, to see at first hand the types of work available for prisoners at one of the most productive and industrially active prisons in the prison estate. Eighty percent of HMP Coldingley's population are from the London area, serving medium- to long-term sentences. One of the criteria that this prison imposes in accepted prisoners transfers is that the prisoners must be willing to work full-time. If prisoners refuse to accept this part of the prison regime, they will be moved on to other prison establishments. . . . The main aim of the prison, as set out in its mission statement, is to increase the employability of prisoners post-release by providing opportunities to address offending behaviour and acquire qualifications and work experience.

We inspected the workshops run at HMP Coldingley, all of which are run as small businesses. The three main industrial workshops, which provide full-time employment for 165 prisoners, are:

1. A general engineering workshop, servicing the [HM] Prison Service and commercial contracts, providing 60 workplaces for prisoners, working 37½ hours per week (half day on Friday).

2. A signs workshop, including a specialist order unit processing contracts as they are received and proceed to completion. The workshop serves the Prison Service, the Ministry of Defence and commercial contracts, providing 54 workplaces for prisoners, working 37½ hours per week.

3. A laundry, providing 60 workplaces for prisoners, turning over £1.2m of commercial contracts and £1m of internal prison work.

Workplace vocational training is delivered alongside the two main workshops, the engineering workshop offering a National Vocational Qualification (NVQ) in production engineering and welding, as well as a forklift driving training course and a signs workshop offering various city and guilds qualifications, including a computer design course. In addition, NVQs are being developed by both the prison cleaning department and the kitchens. The prison also runs an education scheme allowing suitable prisoners day release to attend classes for courses including basic skills (literacy and numeracy), information technology and preparation for work. As part of its resettlement strategy, HMP Coldingley is in process of creating a dedicated job centre to coordinate prisoners' progress during their time at the prison, acting as the main link for both internal and external job markets. The prison is also attempting to establish partnerships with local and national companies.

"We consider that the prison regime should be restructured to support prisoners working a conventional 9 A.M. to 5 P.M. working day."

Coldingley Should Be a Model

The model of HMP Coldingley demonstrates that through a coherent, focused prison work strategy, prisoners can obtain transferable skills and qualifications at the same time as gaining experience of a real working environment and routine. We recommend that the Prison Service develop a prison industrial strategy to ensure that—in the words of the president of the Prison Governors Association—"prison after prison does the same thing and does it in a very businesslike way to very high standards and very competitively".

In one respect only we consider that the Coldingley regime is open to criticism: that it does not allow prisoners to work part-time in order to accommodate other rehabilitative activities such as education, as recommended by the Prison Industries Review. We recommend that in this respect the regime should be modified.

We recommend that the Prison Industries Review recommendation to extend prisoners' working hours should be adopted across the prison estate as a matter of prison policy.

A key performance indicator target should be set requiring individual prison establishments to provide a full working day for prisoners. We consider that the prison regime should be restructured to support prisoners working a conventional 9 A.M. to 5 P.M. working day (in education, vocational training or work programmes, or a mixture of these), fostering the work ethic and giving prisoners responsibility for their future post-release by encouraging them to obtain recognised qualifications and marketable skills through on the job training.

We believe that the Prison Service should make the development of structured work a central part of the national prisons strategy. Every effort should be made to use the Coldingley system as a model for other establishments, adapted as necessary to extend it to those who have little previous experience of work or who are reluctant to take on prison work.

A coherent constructive prison work strategy will not be developed while the responsibility rests on *ad hoc* [not centralized] initiatives by individual prison governors.

The Use of Day Release in Germany

One way of increasing prisoners' employability on release is to permit them to sample the world of work by arrangement with external employers through day release schemes during their imprisonment. We describe below the very extensive use of such day release schemes in Germany.

In England and Wales, prisoners may be released on temporary licence for a number of purposes, including compassionate reasons, training, employment and voluntary work, to re-establish family ties and help prisoners make the transition from prison to life in the community. On most occasions the licences recorded are for one day ('day release'). For resettlement activities [assistance to help prisoners prepare for life after prison], however, the licence may cover up to five days away from the prison. In 2003, over 328,000 temporary licences were issued. Of these, over 50,000 were granted to as-

Proportion of British Prisoners Spending No Time in These Purposeful Activities During the Week

The results are based on a survey of British prisoners conducted by the House of Commons Home Affairs Committee in 2004.

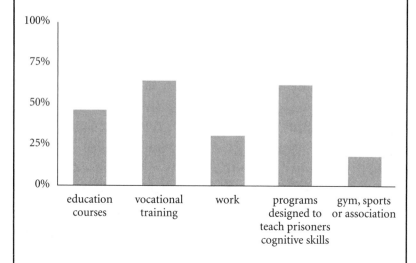

TAKEN FROM: House of Commons Home Affairs Committee, *Rehabilitation of Prisoners: First Report of Session 2004–2005*, London: The Stationery Office Limited, 2005, p. 20.

sist prisoners with resettlement, and over 211,000 were granted to allow prisoners to take part in training, education, community service projects or some form of reparation. In the same year there were only 367 'temporary release failures' (i.e. prisoners on day release absconding).

During our visit to Tegel prison in Germany, we were impressed by the large numbers of prisoners on day release. In Germany, home leaves and other 'relaxations' have become one of the most important features of the contemporary prison system. Since 1977, every prisoner has been entitled to up to 21 days of home leave per year, together with further entitlement to day leaves. Day release for training and work placements are seen as important components of the 'normalisation' principle. The rate of abuse of these entitlements is low: Less than one percent of all prisoners who are granted home leave fail to return unescorted. Reported criminal offences committed during home leaves are relatively rare and usually minor. Denial of home leaves and other relaxations has become an important and effective disciplinary measure.

"Home leave and day release arguably reduce some of the most typical negative consequences of imprisonment: loss of contact with friends and relatives, and ignorance of employment and societal developments."

Sixty percent of all prisoners in Tegel prison are engaged in some form of prison work activity. In recent years, Tegel prison has invested heavily in equipping 14 prison workshops with the technical infrastructure and facilities equivalent in standard to those in the external market place. Whilst the workshops require some level of subsidy, they provide prisoners with directly transferable skills training and work experience.

Once prisoners transfer to all open prison in Germany, they are entitled to day release to attend education and training courses or work placements in the community. Tegel prison runs an extensive Day Release Work Programme. Over 70% of prisoners on the scheme continue to work for their employer after they are released from prison. We have been informed that even those prisoners on temporary work contracts with employers are in the main successful in securing permanent contracts once they demonstrate that they are reliable workers.

Home leave and day release arguably reduce some of the most typical negative consequences of imprisonment: loss of contact with friends and relatives and ignorance of employment and societal developments. We note that prisoners do external work under day release schemes from open prisons on a much greater scale in Germany than in the UK. We recommend that the Prison Service should expand its current system of day release along the lines of the Tegel model set out above, to allow a wider number of prisoners to take part in work and educational programmes in the community as part of their preparation for release. Home leave can provide prisoners with the only chance of sustaining the family unit, and is particularly pertinent to women prisoners, the majority of whom are desperately trying to maintain relationships with children. Save in the most serious cases, there should be a presumption that home leave is available for women prisoners. Day release and home leave plans should become an integral part of the Prison Service's broader resettlement strategy.

Periodical Bibliography

Amnesty International   "Australia: The Impact of Indefinite Detention: The Case to Change Australia's Mandatory Detention Regime," June 29, 2005.

Lorana Bartels   "Suspended Sentences in Tasmania: Key Research Findings," Australian Institute of Criminology, July 2009. www.aic.gov.au.

Canada.com   "Judges Resent 'Implied Criticism' of Mandatory Minimum Sentences: Gomery," November 26, 2007. www.canada.com.

Phil Davison   "Honduran Street Children Face HIV Prison Perils," *Independent*, February 23, 1996.

Sean Duggan   "Criminals with a Mental Illness Need a Prison Break," *Guardian*, July 2, 2009.

Marilyn Elias   "Is Adult Prison Best for Juveniles?" *USA Today*, September 20, 2006.

Frances Harrison   "Saudi Gang-Rape Victim Is Jailed," BBC News, November 15, 2007.

Marc Mauer   Review of *Taking Life Imprisonment Seriously* by Dirk van Zyl Smit, *Federal Sentencing Reporter*, vol. 16, no. 3, February 2004.

On the Docket   "Court to Tackle Life Imprisonment for Juvenile Offenders," May 4, 2009. http://otd.oyez.org.

Parole Board for England and Wales   "History of the Parole Board." www.paroleboard.gov.uk.

Michael Santos   "Prison Reform Should Include Work-Release and Study-Release," Prison News Blog, February 9, 2009.

Chris Togneri   "Study: Incarcerating Youths in Adult Prisons Leads to Abuse, Higher Costs," *Pittsburgh Tribune-Review*, July 29, 2009.

GLOBALVIEWPOINTS

CHAPTER 3

| Prison Conditions

Humane Treatment of Prisoners Is Guaranteed by International Law

J.L. Murdoch

J.L. Murdoch is a professor of public law at the University of Glasgow. In the following viewpoint, Murdoch discusses the legal standards for treatment of prisoners provided under the European Convention on Human Rights. Murdoch especially discusses Article 3 of the convention, which prohibits torture and inhumane or degrading treatment or punishment. According to rulings by the European Court on Human Rights, torture is the term applied to the most severe physical and mental suffering. Murdoch notes that the standards for prisoner treatment have risen over time, and that negligence can in itself constitute a violation of Article 3.

As you read, consider the following questions:

1. What case provided the key definitions of torture, inhumane treatment, and degrading treatment?

2. Which was the first case in which the European Court on Human Rights found that state action had amounted to torture?

3. According to the European Court on Human Rights, is rape of a detainee in itself enough to constitute torture?

The risk of ill-treatment in detention is rarely remote. At the point of deprivation of liberty and when the support of family and friends may be needed most, the social isolation a detainee finds himself in brings with it a particular risk of inappropriate state action. It is generally recognised that a detainee is at his most vulnerable at the very outset of loss of liberty, and that this vulnerability may be exploited by state officials with a view to extracting information or a confession. To help counteract this situation, much emphasis is placed in European standards upon the importance of the selection and training of state officials such as police officers and prison staff in the prevention of ill-treatment. However, where the commitment of the state's leadership to combating impunity is ambiguous in relation to certain classes of detainee or in certain circumstances, delivery of the message that there must be "zero tolerance" of torture and other forms of ill-treatment by law-enforcement personnel will be undermined. Yet eradication of the deliberate infliction of torture will still rely to a large extent upon judicial safeguards and upon the international condemnation that a finding of a violation of Article 2 [of the European Convention on Human Rights, which requires respect for the right to life] or Article 3 [which prohibits torture and inhumane or degrading treatment] is likely to occasion.

Article 3 Prohibits Torture and Inhumane or Degrading Treatment of Prisoners

There are two essential questions in the application of Article 3: First, does the treatment or punishment complained of meet the minimum level of suffering required to give rise to application of Article 3; and second, if this threshold test is satisfied, what is the appropriate label to be applied to the treatment or punishment? The first question needs to be considered with care. The main principles are easy enough to restate. The punishment or treatment complained of must constitute a minimum level of severity as assessed by reference to the circumstances of the "treatment" or punishment in question including its duration and its physical and mental effects as well as the sex, age and health of the victim, and only suffering which is considered excessive in the light of prevailing general standards will meet this threshold test. The absence of any evidence of a positive intention to humiliate or to debase an individual does not rule out a finding of a violation of Article 3. Further, it is not merely direct or actual victims of ill-treatment who may rely upon the guarantee, for even failing actual infliction of any such treatment, the threat of ill-treatment may also trigger Article 3 consideration providing it is "sufficiently real and immediate", so that the threat of torture itself may be enough to constitute a violation of Article 3. In assessing whether Article 3's threshold has been reached, the whole range of issues and circumstances arising in each case must be taken into account.

"The threat of torture itself may be enough to constitute a violation of Article 3 [which prohibits inhumane treatment]."

When these principles are applied to concrete facts, however, there is . . . often a sense in which the conclusions [of the European Court of Human Rights] appear subjective and impressionistic. The stringency with which the jurisprudence proclaims that any unnecessary use of force against a detainee will involve a breach of the guarantee (as in *Ribitsch v. Austria*) can be contrasted with the apparent lack of concern to prevent unnecessary humiliation through the handcuffing of a detainee in public (as in *Raninen v. Finland*); and the condemnation of the failure to provide clean underwear (as in *Hurtado v. Switzerland*) seems at odds with the failure to appreciate the concerns of a "lonely and insecure 7-year-old boy" subjected to corporal punishment (as in *Costello-Roberts v. the United Kingdom*). That the threshold set in different cases can vary is, though, not surprising: Much will turn on the assumptions, experiences, values and prejudices of the members of the court. . . .

The Definition of Torture, Inhuman Treatment, and Degrading Treatment

The question of the appropriate label to be given to treatment or punishment meeting the threshold test is determined by assessment of the severity of the treatment, and thus the distinctions between "torture", "inhuman" and "degrading treatment or punishment" reflect differences in the intensity of suffering and assessment of state purpose as judged by contemporary standards. The key definitions were provided in the case of *Ireland v. the United Kingdom*, a case involving the infliction of the so-called "five techniques" on suspects in interrogation centres. The treatment complained of had involved wall-standing (forcing the detainees to remain for periods of some hours in a stress position), hooding (placing a dark bag over the detainees' heads for lengthy periods), subjection to "white noise", deprivation of sleep and deprivation of food and drink. The key passage in the judgment concerns the interpretation to be given to each concept:

> The five techniques were applied in combination, with premeditation and for hours at a stretch; they caused, if not actual bodily injury, at least intense physical and mental suffering to the persons subjected thereto and also led to acute psychiatric disturbances during interrogation. They accordingly fell into the category of inhuman treatment within the meaning of Article 3. The techniques were also degrading since they were such as to arouse in their victims feelings of fear, anguish and inferiority capable of humiliating and debasing them and possibly breaking their physical or moral resistance. . . . In order to determine whether the five techniques should also be qualified as torture, the court must

have regard to the distinction, embodied in Article 3, between this notion and that of inhuman or degrading treatment.

In the court's view, this distinction derives principally from a difference in the intensity of the suffering inflicted. The court considers in fact that, whilst there exists on the one hand violence which is to be condemned both on moral grounds and also in most cases under the domestic law of the contracting states but which does not fall within Article 3 of the convention [European Convention on Human Rights], it appears on the other hand that it was the intention that the convention, with its distinction between "torture" and "inhuman or degrading treatment", should by the first of these terms attach a special stigma to deliberate inhuman treatment causing very serious and cruel suffering.

The Difference Between Torture and Inhuman Treatment

It is useful to reiterate these definitions in the judgment. "Torture" is reserved for the most serious forms of violation of Article 3. The term thus attaches a "special stigma to deliberate inhuman treatment causing very serious and cruel suffering". In contrast, "inhuman" treatment or punishment involves the infliction of intense physical and mental suffering. Of crucial importance in this case, though, was the determination that the "five techniques" had not amounted to "torture":

> Although the five techniques, as applied in combination, undoubtedly amounted to inhuman and degrading treatment, although their object was the extraction of confessions, the naming of others and/or information and although they were used systematically, they did not occasion suffering of the particular intensity and cruelty implied by the word torture as so understood.

This approach also proceeds upon degrees of severity rather than upon purpose. . . . However, more recently the court has accepted that consideration of state motive or purpose in assessing the level of violation may indeed be relevant, the court is beginning to develop an alternative (or at least a parallel) approach which adopts the stricter test of the United Nations Convention Against Torture. The first court ruling that state action had amounted to "torture", *Aksoy v. Turkey*, illustrates this. The applicant had been stripped naked by police officers and then suspended by his arms which had been tied behind his back. This had involved severe pain and subsequent temporary paralysis of both arms; its deliberate infliction had also required "a certain amount of preparation and exertion" by state officials; and its purpose appeared to have been to extract information or a confession from the applicant. Infliction of ill-treatment may thus be considered as aggravated when it is premeditated or inflicted for a particular purpose such as to extract a confession or information.

"Infliction of ill-treatment may thus be considered as aggravated when it is premeditated or inflicted for a particular purpose such as to extract a confession or information."

Degrading Treatment

The least serious trading of a violation of Article 3 will involve degrading treatment or punishment. "Degrading" treatment or punishment, according to the *Ireland v. the United Kingdom* judgment, is that which is "designed to arouse in the victims feelings of fear, anguish and inferiority capable of humiliating and debasing them and possibly breaking their physical or moral resistance", or in other words . . . as driving the victim to act against his will or conscience. State motive is also a relevant factor. Thus in determining whether treatment is "degrading", the court will "have regard to whether its object is to humiliate and debase the person concerned and

The CIA Tortured Prisoners in Europe

A large number of Polish and American intelligence operatives have . . . gone on record that the CIA [Central Intelligence Agency] maintained a prison in northeastern Poland. Independent of these sources, Polish government officials from the Justice and Defense Ministry have also reported that the Americans had a secret base near Szymany airport. And so began on March 7, 2003, one of the darkest chapters of recent American—and European—history.

It was apparently here, just under an hour's drive from Szymany airport, that [Khalid] Sheikh Mohammed was tortured, exactly 183 times with waterboarding—an interrogation technique that simulates the sensation of drowning—in March 2003 alone. That averages out to eight times a day. And all of this happened right here in Europe. . . .

Sheikh Mohammed said that they cut the clothes from his body, photographed him naked and threw him in a three-by-four-meter (10 x 13 ft) cell with wooden walls. That was when the hardest phase of the interrogating began, he claims. . . .

He says he was questioned roughly eight hours a day. He spent the first month naked and standing, with his hands chained to the ceiling of the cell, even at night. They led them into another room for questioning, he says. That's where the bed stood that he says he was strapped to for waterboarding.

John Goetz and Britta Sandberg,
"New Evidence of Torture Prison in Poland,"
Spiegel Online, *April 27, 2009. www.speigel.de.*

whether, as far as the consequences are concerned, it adversely affected his or her personality in a manner incompatible with Article 3". . . .

There is another crucial factor to consider in reading Article 3 case law. In regard to the deliberate ill-treatment of detainees, the importance of . . . current expectations is apparent, for earlier judgments may need to be read with some care as heightened standards may now more readily lead to the conclusion that certain ill-treatment now indeed justifies the application of the label of "torture". For example, in *Selmouni v. France*, the applicant had been held in police custody for some three days during which he had been beaten with a baseball bat or similar implement, urinated upon and sexually assaulted. For the court, this had involved particularly serious and cruel physical and mental treatment now deserving to be regarded as "torture":

[H]aving regard to the fact that the convention [European Convention on Human Rights] is a "living instrument which must be interpreted in the light of present-day conditions", the court considers that certain acts which were classified in the past as "inhuman and degrading treatment" as opposed to "torture" could be classified differently in future. It takes the view that the increasingly high standard being required in the area of the protection of human rights and fundamental liberties correspondingly and inevitably requires greater firmness in assessing breaches of the fundamental values of democratic societies.

"Ill-conceived or thoughtless action on the part of state authorities may similarly be condemned as unwarranted excesses."

This reiteration of heightened expectations and a more critical approach to ill-treatment is also evidenced in cases such as *Aydin v. Turkey* where a 17-year-old Kurdish girl had been stripped, beaten, sprayed with cold water and subsequently raped by soldiers. Since the detention had been with a view to interrogation, the suffering inflicted was to be considered as having been calculated to serve the same purpose. For the court, while the infliction of a series of "particularly terrifying and humiliating experiences" would have in itself constituted "torture", the infliction of rape upon a detainee in itself was certainly also enough to do so:

> Rape of a detainee by an official of the State must be considered to be an especially grave and abhorrent form of ill-treatment given the ease with which the offender can exploit the vulnerability and weakened resistance of his victim. Furthermore, rape leaves deep psychological scars on the victim which do not respond to the passage of time as quickly as other forms of physical and mental violence. The applicant also experienced the acute physical pain of forced penetration, which must have left her feeling debased and violated both physically and emotionally.

Negligence Is Also Prohibited by Article 3

The cases discussed involve the deliberate infliction of ill-treatment, but ill-conceived or thoughtless action on the part of state authorities may similarly be condemned as unwarranted excesses. In *Henaf v. France*, for example, an elderly prisoner, whom the authorities considered could be adequately guarded while in hospital for a throat operation by two prison officers without the need to be handcuffed, had nevertheless been kept in handcuffs since his arrival at the hospital the day before his operation; that night, he had been shackled to his bed by a chain attached to one of his ankles which had resulted in such pain that he had found sleep impossible. In consequence, he had no option other than to insist that the operation be postponed until after he had been released from prison. In determining that the applicant had been subjected to inhuman treatment, the court took into account factors including his age and state of health, the absence of antecedents giving rise to a serious fear of a risk to security, and the prison governor's written instructions that the applicant was to be given normal (rather than special) supervision which in any case had involved the stationing of officers outside his room. In short, the disproportionate response in the light of actual requirements of security had been such as to meet the minimum level of severity for a violation of Article 3.

In France, Prison Conditions Are Deteriorating

Jean-Marc Rouillan

Jean-Marc Rouillan, a leader of the Action Directe urban guerrilla group, spent twenty years in prison for the murder of the CEO of Renault and a defense ministry official. Rouillan is the author of Chroniques Carcérales, *an account of his time in prison. In the following viewpoint, Rouillan argues that French prisons are overcrowded and rely more on force, brutality, and solitary confinement than in the past. Prison services have also been cut, and prisoners are forced to pay more for basic necessities. Rouillan argues that such unfair treatment of prisoners will have a negative impact on society as a whole.*

As you read, consider the following questions:

1. According to Jean-Marc Rouillan, why are prisoners refusing to leave their cells for medical treatment?
2. According to Rouillan, for what reason does the management at the Moulins prison sometimes put someone in solitary confinement?
3. What is the upper limit on prisoners' savings accounts before an extra 10 percent of gross pay goes straight into a compensation scheme?

Jean-Marc Rouillan, "France: Return of the Convicts," translated by Harry Forster, *Le Monde Diplomatique*, July 2005. Copyright © 1997–2008 *Le Monde Diplomatique*. This article reprinted from *Le Monde Diplomatique*'s English language version, available online at www.mondediplo.com. Reproduced by permission.

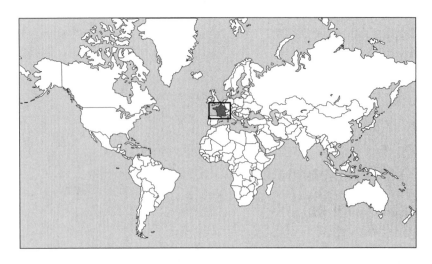

Conditions in France's prisons have severely deteriorated in the past decade. The recommendations of parliamentary committees and well-meaning statements by charities have done nothing to slow, let alone halt, the downward trend. Recent government measures to tighten discipline are worsening an intolerable situation. The current policy is based on the beliefs that prison is the cure for all ills and that authority must be restored.

Prisons Are Overcrowded

Despite the different language, it is easy to identify the simplistic ideas of United States conservatives at work. With increasing use of casual labour in the workplace and zero tolerance in the courts, prisons are again a crucial mechanism for protecting society from the "dangerous classes", which particularly means those in the most vulnerable circumstances. Never, since the bad old days of deportation [when French prisoners were sent to prison in a French colony such as Guiana], has prison policy played so essential a role in social segregation.

One of the most obvious results is overpopulation. Despite drives to release selected prisoners and build new prisons, France's jails are bursting. In the naïve conviction that harsh sentencing will cut delinquency, courts are packing jails with new inmates. There have never been so many people in prison, sentenced or on remand. Never have penalties been so severe. Never have there been so many life sentences.

Observers have criticised problems caused by overcrowding. But even the best informed people on the outside do not realise what that really means. When they talk about the difficulties of three or four prisoners sharing a nine-metre-square cell, they overlook the side effects: There is less time and fewer resources for everything, visits, showers, social activities, exercise, which impacts on the quality of meals and medical care, and aggravates unemployment. Overcrowding, which affects every aspect of daily life behind bars, makes everything worse for inmates.

"Physical and mental violence now play a bigger part in the running of prisons to keep a potentially explosive situation under control and quell thoughts of resistance."

Force in Prisons Is Increasing

Two other features of the current changes attract less media attention but are far-reaching. The use of force as a means of asserting authority and financial pressure on prisoners are on the rise.

Physical and mental violence now play a bigger part in the running of prisons to keep a potentially explosive situation under control and quell thoughts of resistance. In February 2003 France's justice minister, Dominique Perben, set up regional intervention and security teams (ERIS); this sent a powerful message to all prison officers. Since then beatings have increased, without attracting any attention in the media or the courts. A duty of ERIS units is to supervise prison searches. These high-profile operations have never produced convincing results, but provide an excuse for punitive expeditions and collective punishment after attempted breakouts or minor incidents.

Since autumn 2004 there has been an atmosphere of physical confrontation. At Lannemezan [a prison in southern France where Rouillan was incarcerated] more and more guards go on duty in combat gear. Use of handcuffs (a symptomatic gesture) is widespread. In the solitary wing at Fleury-Mérogis, a huge prison south of Paris, prisoners are cuffed US-style [putting their hands through the bars of the cell to be handcuffed before the door is opened] for any movements inside or outside buildings. Handcuffs seem to have become standard equipment. In the prison hospital the senior supervisor for each floor wears handcuffs and riot gloves on his belt, although 90% of patients cannot get out of bed unassisted.

In December 2003 the story of a woman at Fleury-Mérogis kept handcuffed while she gave birth prompted an outcry. But there was much less response a year later when the ministry issued instructions that all patients should not only be restrained, but handcuffed behind their backs. Whenever they go to court, or anywhere else outside, detainees spend several hours cuffed in prison vans. You can only understand the pain if you have experienced this treatment. So prisoners are refusing to leave their cells for medical treatment.

The Use of Solitary Confinement Is Increasing

Besides this daily brutality, there are solitary confinement and transfers to other units for disciplinary reasons. No one is safe from the threat of physical violence or solitary confinement. Anyone thought to be a troublemaker or a potential ringleader is a target. As happened in the days of the dreaded top-security detention centres (QHS, *quartier haute sécurité*) selected hard cases are often rotated from unit to unit. About 200 supposedly dangerous prisoners travel back and forth between the solitary wings of prisons all over France, two months in Épinal, two weeks in Grasse, four months in Perpignan. Some places are mandatory stages in this progress, and the tough conditions in them are designed to break people. The former QHS at Fleury-Mérogis, which reopened last year, is typical. Like similar units in Paris, Rouen and Lyon, it is set aside for convicts accused of attempting or carrying out violent escapes.

The isolation wings of large prisons are packed. In the past, space was reserved for the worst psychiatric cases and prisoners under official protection. But now inmates may find themselves in solitary for varying periods of time for no good reason. At Moulins, the management may put someone in solitary simply to make room for a new arrival. Due to the shortage of isolation facilities, a prisoner may be put in an ordinary cell, but the door will only be opened in the presence of a senior officer with an extra escort. Those subjected to this treatment are only allowed an hour's exercise a day in an inner courtyard. Much of their personal kit and televisions or radios are confiscated. Access to showers is restricted and all the other usual activities—telephone, laundry, sport, library—are prohibited.

"With the further decline in the quality of meals, a black market for food has sprung up in some jails; this has not happened for a long time."

Prison Services Are Being Cut

It seems to have become deliberate prison policy to cut the standard of living of inmates and reduce the range of services available to them. This operates together with a drive to extort as much money as possible from those serving sentences; the official reason is the need to boost the finances of criminal injuries compensation schemes. The prison service has launched economy drives, shelving free services and basic supplies. This

French Prisons Are More Crowded than Others in Europe

It's an especially hot summer in French jails. In July [2008], the number of detainees hit 64,250 people—the highest number since World War II, when jails were crowded with accused Nazi collaborators. Worse: The prisons are operating at 126 percent of capacity—far higher than the European average—with some French jails housing twice as many inmates as there is room for. Seven in 10 prisoners are living in overcrowded conditions.

Tracy McNicoll, "Incarceration Nation,"
Newsweek Online, *August 2, 2008. www.newsweek.com.*

process has affected social activities. Damaged or worn-out equipment is no longer replaced and only the bare minimum is done to maintain collective areas. When the old social centre at Moulins closed, management gave prisoners the run of a group of cells that had been closed for 10 years, but they had to pay for repairs and decorating, including light bulbs.

To cover everyday needs prisoners must buy everything from bin-liners [plastic liners for wastebaskets] to drugs prescribed by prison doctors. With the further decline in the quality of meals, a black market for food has sprung up in some jails; this has not happened for a long time. To survive, inmates must buy items of food and personal hygiene. But canteen prices are exorbitant, some 30%–50% higher than prices in shops.

The aim of this policy is to make detainees pay for their upkeep, while forcing them to accept tougher working conditions. Having allowed free social and education activities to die out, the prison service now deducts from prisoners' pay more than a third of the amount allocated to training schemes organised by the ministry of education and prisoners' aid groups.

The prison service benefits on all counts, particularly as it has just changed the rules. Several provisions of the new rules on prisoner resources introduced in October 2004 contribute to the growing poverty of inmates. Since a law on prisons was passed in 1975 the amount that prisoners can earn in a month without paying social charges has risen only from €183 [euros] to €200. Over the same period deductions on any excess income have tripled, and are now 30%. To make matters worse, earnings are now lumped together with any money orders received from outside. This automatically results in a 20%–35% rise in deductions and a proportional drop in income from work.

> *"French prisons have always brought out the baser instincts in humanity, in relations between prisoners, and between them and the prison service and courts. Hypocrisy is the prime quality."*

Contrary to recommendations by parliamentary committees, pay for work in prison has not improved. The worst abuses involve piecework reminiscent of the 19th century, often done under health and safety conditions that disregard current regulations.

Prisons Extort Money from Prisoners

The new rules fix an upper limit of €1,000 on prisoners' saving accounts. This means that when savings reach this target, an extra 10% of gross pay goes straight into a compensation scheme. Until now prisoners serving long sentences could save several thousand euros, to have some finance on release. Given the lack of any real welfare service they rightly assume it is wisest to be able to fend for themselves. But when they get outside without work or a home, and no more than €1,000 to tide them over the first three months, after which they qualify for basic welfare coverage, what choice do they have? It is hardly a recipe for keeping past offenders out of trouble.

The government has also introduced a form of legal blackmail rooted in the worst traditions of retribution. The courts, prison service and ministry criminologists believe that if a prisoner voluntarily pays money he or she has accomplished an act of expiation signifying acceptance of the sentence. In the past believers washed away their sins by paying for a mass to be celebrated. In our world prisoners demonstrate their redemption by paying hard-earned cash. In its correspondence with prisoners the parole board puts a clear price on more favourable terms. A €15 contribution to a compensation scheme buys an extra day on temporary release. An undertaking to pay €30 a month knocks a month off the sentence.

French prisons have always brought out the baser instincts in humanity, in relations between prisoners, and between them and the prison service and courts. Hypocrisy is the prime quality. Treachery and lies are always rewarded. Here is a story that shows how these may be used to pay fines and compensate injuries. Two inmates of a prison in the south of France, whose sentences were due to come up for review, began to refuse to work in the prison workshop. Under no illusions about the attitude of the parole board, they dealt drugs from their cells to raise funds for the compensation scheme. Their trade was highly profitable and they were able to negotiate a reduction in sentence and early release. A few months later a non-French prisoner ran into financial difficulties. Besides endless working, he had been voluntarily repaying €100 a month in compensation. But problems at home suddenly prevented further repayments. The board refused to allow for his difficulties and docked a month from his early release package for failing to comply with the compensation contract.

Society will pay dearly for such short-sighted policies.

Turkey's Torture of Prisoners May Be Changing

Mustafa Akyol

Mustafa Akyol is a Turkish Muslim writer based in Istanbul. He is opinion editor and columnist for Turkish Daily News. *In the following viewpoint, Akyol argues that Turkey has long had a tradition of abuse by security forces and police. Though things have improved since the 1990s, Akyol says that police continue to torture and even murder those in their custody, such as Engin Çeber who died in police custody in 2008. Çeber's death, however, did result in an official government apology. Akyol hopes that this apology suggests that the Turkish government is serious about its pledges to eliminate torture.*

As you read, consider the following questions:

1. Why did many people in Turkey denounce the 1978 movie *Midnight Express*?
2. According to Mustafa Akyol, how many nights did Engin Çeber spend in police custody?
3. What did Justice Minister Mehmet Ali Şahin do to the officials implicated in the death of Çeber?

When the movie *Midnight Express* made headlines in 1978, many Turks were quite angry. The film presented Turkey's prisons as slices of hell and many people here denounced it as "anti-Turkish propaganda."

Mustafa Akyol, "Torture as Usual—But a First-Time Apology," *Turkish Daily News*, October 16, 2008. Reproduced by permission of Gina Maccoby Literary Agency.

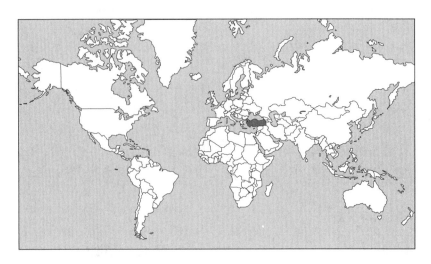

Turkey Has Been Notorious for Torture

I was too young to understand such matters then. But I grew up a little and watched *Midnight Express* in the early 1990s, when it was, for the first time, shown on Turkish television. (Before that, it was banned.) And unlike most of my countrymen, I was not offended by its content.

Yes, it was apparently exaggerating the conditions that Billy Hayes, the main character who was imprisoned in Istanbul for smuggling hashish, faced in Turkish courts and prisons. But the main message of the film was bitterly true: Turkey is a country where torture had been a systematic function of the "security forces." It used to be so bad that how to protect yourself from these "security forces" had become the main concern for millions of citizens.

So, instead of lashing out against *Midnight Express*, we Turks should have lashed out against our iron-handed state, which has brutally tortured so many people. Especially during the dark periods of military coups, but also in "normal" times, the Turkish police, gendarmerie and other men in arms have done terrible, awful, evil things. This has not just traumatized and ended lives, it also consolidated the very thing that the state wanted to carve out: political, and sometimes violent, opposition. It is well-known that the outlawed PKK (the Kurdistan Workers' Party) [a militant organization dedicated to creating an independent Kurdish state] had its biggest recruitment among the victims of the infamous Diyarbakir Military Prison. The tortures the inmates went through in that wicked place were unbelievable. The PKK's terrorist reaction would be unbelievable, too.

"Turkey is a country where torture had been a systematic function of the 'security forces.'"

Police in Turkey Still Use Torture

Now, to be fair, Turkey has made some progress from that point of ultimate brutality. Since the late '90s, mostly thanks to the European Union-driven reforms, torture has been decreased and security forces have become more transparent and responsible. The police are actually trying to erase their bad image by launching public relations campaigns. Police stations present posters of smiling cops. And I have personally met young and kind officers who sincerely believe in a democratic, free, and torture-less Turkey.

But, as in other cases, old habits apparently die hard. And the Turkish security forces can still be a threat to the rights and lives of Turkish citizens, as evidenced by the recent tragedy of Engin Çeber.

Mr. Çeber, a young left-wing political activist, was arrested on September 29 [2008] in Istanbul, while protesting against the shooting of one of his comrades, Ferhat Gerçek, for simply selling a leftist journal. Mr. Çeber, along with three other activists, spent nine nights in custody, in first the Istinye police station and then Metris prison. Then he was taken to Şişli Etfal Hospital, where he died two days later. The cause of his death was a "brain hemorrhage," which clearly implies that he was beaten to death by the police.

This is so Turkish police as usual. I remember many cases like this over the years, in which the police beat their captives to death and then reported that they committed suicide. Some police files are so bizarre that they say things like "the detainee suddenly started to hit his head against the wall and we couldn't stop him."

Just yesterday another incident took place in Istanbul, which again pointed to the sad fact that some of our policemen are actually sadistic brutes. As reported by daily *Milliyet*, an undercover police asked for tea in a teahouse in the Kartal district. He didn't like the shape of the cups, so he didn't want to pay. After a heated discussion, this police and his friends started beating the poor shop owner. His skull is reported to have been broken because the police put him to the ground and crushed his head with their feet.

"I remember many cases like this over the years, in which the police beat their captives to death and then reported that they committed suicide."

An Apology Gives Hope

To date, very few police officers have been sentenced for such crimes. The general mind-set of the courts, and the bureaucracy, was that these were patriotic guys who were doing their job but who had gone a little bit too far. To kill and persecute for the sake of the state, Turkey's national idol, was deemed tolerable.

Yet, as I have said before, things have been slowly changing and a first happened right after the death of Engin Çeber. Justice Minister Mehmet Ali Şahin not only suspended the 19 officials, including two prison officers, one senior officer and the prison doctor who filed a report on Çeber's condition without seeing him. He also said this:

Torture in Iranian Prisons

Zahra Bani Yaqub [alternatively spelled Ya'qub or Yaghoub] ... was a young [Iranian] doctor with a bright future.

But last October, Bani Yaqub was arrested while walking in a park in the western city of Hamadan.... The next day, she was dead.

Police say she committed suicide in prison overnight, but her family ... accuse[s] prison authorities of killing Bani Yaqub, whose case is merely the latest in a series of suspicious deaths or tortures in prison to be highlighted by human rights activists.

Farangis Najibullah,
"Iran: Human Rights Activists Concerned over
Prison Deaths, Torture," Radio Free Europe/Radio Liberty,
February 17, 2008. www.rferl.org

"I, in the name of my state and government, apologize to [Engin Çeber's] loved ones. We will leave no stone unturned in finding all those responsible."

Of course no apology will compensate for the tragic loss of the Çeber family. But it is still meaningful that a state official apologizes to a family in the name of the state. This is a society which is brainwashed to believe that the state is a sacred entity which never does anything wrong. For some Turks, actually, the state has become the definition of what is right and what is wrong.

Time has come to change that. And although I am not holding my breath, I am still hoping the AKP (Justice and Development Party) government will be steadfast in their "zero tolerance" to torture policy. Their own experience with the Turkish state [before the party achieved power in 2007] must have taught them that this Leviathan desperately needs to be tamed.

Zimbabwe's Prison Conditions Are Horrible

Jonathan Clayton

Jonathan Clayton is the Africa correspondent for London's Times; *he was imprisoned and tortured before his release by Zimbabwe authorities in 2008. In the following viewpoint, Clayton discusses a new documentary about Zimbabwe's prisons called* Hell Hole. *The documentary shows horrible conditions including overcrowding, mass starvation, and dead bodies lying unattended in the cells. Rates of HIV infection and tuberculosis are also dangerously high. Clayton explains that President Robert Mugabe's failure to resign following election losses plunged Zimbabwe into chaos with disastrous results for prisoners.*

As you read, consider the following questions:

1. In what country was the documentary *Hell Hole* initially broadcast?

2. How many deaths were reported in just one of the prisons in Bulawayo in March 2005, according to Jonathan Clayton?

3. According to some reports, how many prisoners in Zimbabwe are HIV positive?

Jonathan Clayton, "Zimbabwe Prisoners in 'Hell on Earth' Die from Disease and Hunger," *Times Online*, April 1, 2009. Copyright © 2009 Times Newspapers Ltd. Reproduced by permission.

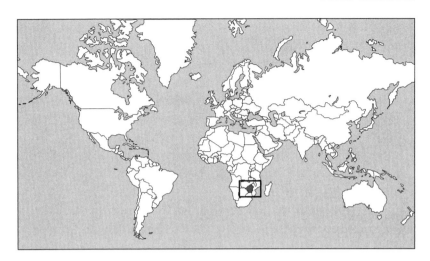

A horrifying investigative film, shot undercover in Zimbabwe, has exposed how prisons under President [Robert] Mugabe have become death camps for thousands of inmates who are deprived of food and medical care.

The documentary, shown last night [May 31, 2009] on South Africa's state broadcaster SABC, documented the "living hell" for prisoners across 55 state institutions. The result, *Hell Hole*, was a grim account of a crisis in which dozens of inmates die each day.

Starvation and Death Plague Zimbabwe Prisons

Describing the conditions in two of the main prisons in the capital, Harare, in late 2008, a prison officer said: "We have gone the whole year in which—for prisoners and prison officers—the food is hand-to-mouth. They'll be lucky to get one meal. Sometimes they will sleep without. We have moving skeletons, moving graves. They're dying."

The film was made by SABC's *Special Assignment* programme and shot over three months with cameras smuggled into the prisons. Reaction in South Africa, where the authori-

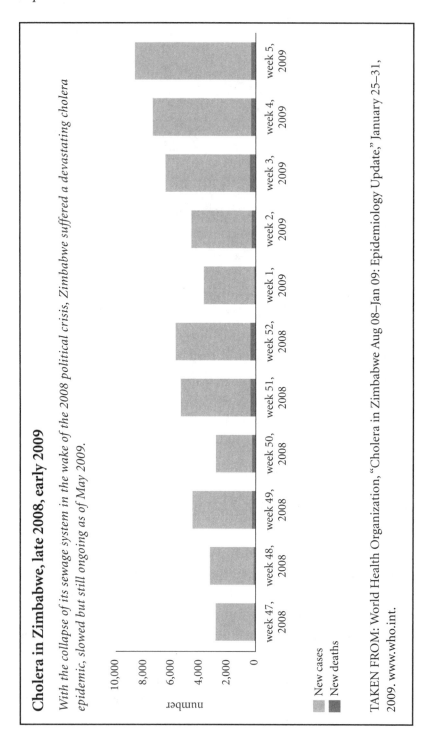

Cholera in Zimbabwe, late 2008, early 2009

With the collapse of its sewage system in the wake of the 2008 political crisis, Zimbabwe suffered a devastating cholera epidemic, slowed but still ongoing as of May 2009.

New cases
New deaths

TAKEN FROM: World Health Organization, "Cholera in Zimbabwe Aug 08–Jan 09: Epidemiology Update," January 25–31, 2009. www.who.int.

ties try to deny the extent of the crisis in its neighbour [Zimbabwe], is certain to be fierce.

The film showed how prison staff have converted cells and storage rooms to "hospital wards" for the dying and makeshift mortuaries, where bodies "rotted on the floor with maggots moving all around". They have had to create mass graves within prison grounds to accommodate the dead. In many prisons the dead took over whole cells and competed for space with the living. Prisoners described how the sick and the healthy slept side by side, packed together like sardines, along with those who died in the night.

Prisoners in the film are suffering from slow starvation, nutrition-related illnesses and an array of other diseases to which they are exposed as a result of living in unhygienic conditions.

"Prisoners described how the sick and the healthy slept side by side, packed together like sardines, along with those who died in the night."

A former prisoner, a young man, struggled to convey the horror of these conditions: "That place, I haven't got the words . . . I can describe it as hell on earth—though they say it's more than hell." In October last year [2008] the Zimbabwe Association for Crime Prevention and Rehabilitation of the Offender (ZACRO) released a report noting that there were 55 prisons in Zimbabwe, with the capacity to hold 17,000 inmates. But in October 2008 it was estimated that more than 35,000 people were in jail.

Zimbabwe's Turmoil Is Responsible for the Prison Conditions

A report released to accompany the film said that unlike Zimbabweans on the outside, "inmates can't beg for food from passersby, they can't forage for wild berries in the bush, and they can't rummage through dustbins for waste food.

"Because of this, Zimbabwe's prisons constitute a unique and especially cruel form of torture," said the report compiled by a human rights organisation called Sokwanele, or "Enough is Enough". The number of deaths from disease in the prisons has risen since the start of the economic decline and political crisis that has gripped the country since the late 1990s.

"Unlike Zimbabweans on the outside, 'inmates can't beg for food from passersby, they can't forage for wild berries in the bush, and they can't rummage through dustbins for waste food.'"

From 1998 to 2000 the Zimbabwe Prison Service estimated that there were some 300 deaths each year because of disease, with tuberculosis the biggest killer. In May 2004 a senior prison officer reported 15 deaths a week, and a peak of 130 deaths in March of that year, in just one of the prisons in Zimbabwe's second city, Bulawayo.

Since then the crisis has deteriorated greatly as all the country's services have entered meltdown after Mr. Mugabe's refusal to leave office in the wake of rigged polls [in 2008].

The *Times* spent ten days in one of the "better" prisons in Bulawayo last year [2008], surrounded by young skeletal men who fought over small plates of sadza (local maize), and noted severe overcrowding, overflowing toilets, water and electricity cuts, and a lack of blankets and basic commodities such as soap. Those without people on the outside to bring them food face almost certain starvation unless they find another solution such as resorting to prostitution.

Prison populations also have high rates of HIV/AIDS infection, with some reports estimating that more than half of prisoners are HIV positive. Antiretrovirals are unavailable and the dietary requirements of treatment cannot be met in any case.

There are few drugs for the treatment of tuberculosis and other diseases, and the cramped and filthy conditions ease the transmission of infection. Late last year [2008] and early this year [2009] a cholera outbreak in Harare's Central Prison killed four to five prisoners each day, with a peak of 18 deaths in one day, according to prison officers.

In South African Prisons, Rape Is Widespread

Just Detention International

Just Detention International (JDI) is a human rights organization that seeks to end sexual abuse in all forms of detention. In the following viewpoint, JDI reports that overcrowding, widespread gang activity, and poor prison policies have contributed to chronic sexual abuse in South African prisons. This problem is especially serious because of the high rates of HIV/AIDS in South African prisons. JDI says that the recent parliamentary redefinition of rape as a gender-neutral crime and a move toward independent oversight of prisons could help address the problem.

As you read, consider the following questions:

1. In South African prisons, what is the system of "lock-up"?
2. According to JDI, how many prisoners in South Africa are released back into the community each year?
3. In what year did South Africa's parliament establish a gender neutral definition of rape?

South African detention facilities are plagued by sexual abuse, in contravention of domestic law and international human rights principles. The country's prisons tend to be

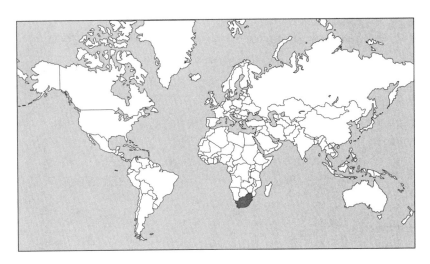

overcrowded, and suffer from high levels of violence and poor management. Pre-trial detainees, first-time, non-violent offenders, and those who are gay or transgender, physically small or mentally disabled are among the most likely targets of sexual abuse. Gangs play an integral role in perpetuating sexual violence in South Africa's prisons.

Gangs and Prison Policy Contribute to Rapes

In 2006, the Jali Commission of Inquiry, appointed by former President Thabo Mbeki, described "the horrific scourge of sexual violence that plagues [South African] prisons where appalling abuses and acts of sexual perversion are perpetrated on helpless and unprotected prisoners." Young inmates are especially vulnerable to being viewed by more powerful prisoners as commodities to be sold or traded. One nationwide South African prison gang—known as the '28s'—uses rape as a means to recruit and control so-called 'wyfies,' who are forced to provide sex and domestic services to other gang members. While the 28s is most often associated with rape and forced prison 'marriages,' all of the dominant gangs, in-

149

Estimated Percentage of South Africans with HIV, 2005		
Age (years)	Male %	Female %
2–4	4.9	5.3
5–9	4.2	4.8
10–14	1.6	1.8
15–19	3.2	9.4
20–24	6.0	23.9
25–29	12.1	33.3
30–34	23.3	26.0
35–39	23.3	19.3
40–44	17.5	12.4
45–49	10.3	8.7
50–54	14.2	7.5
55–59	6.4	3.0
60+	4.0	3.7
Total	8.2	13.3

TAKEN FROM: AVERT, "South Africa: HIV & AIDS Statistics," April 14, 2009. www.avert.org.

cluding the two other so-called numbers gangs (the '26s' and '27s') are also involved in sexual abuse.

Fueling the incidence of sexual violence in South African prisons are ineffectual and detrimental corrections policies. Because inmates are not properly classified, those most vulnerable to sexual violence are commonly housed with predatory gang members in large communal cells. Perhaps the most problematic practice in prisons throughout South Africa is the system of "lock-up." Each afternoon, inmates are provided their dinner in a paper bag and sent to their cells, mostly large dormitories, at which point these housing units are locked until the next morning. During the late afternoon, evening, and throughout the night, the prisons operate with a minimal staff, leaving inmates to fend for themselves. It is during lock-up that the vast majority of sexual assaults in South African prisons occur.

Prison Rape Exacerbates the AIDS Crisis

Rape in South African prisons is directly linked to the country's HIV/AIDS crisis. HIV prevalence in South Africa is among the highest in the world, and the rate among prisoners is estimated to be more than double that of the general population. The Jali Commission concluded that, in light of the egregious sexual abuses in prisons nationwide, the national Department of Correctional Services (DCS) "is effectively, by omission, imposing a death sentence on vulnerable prisoners." With 360,000 prisoners in South Africa released back into their communities each year, the consequences for the public are dire as well.

Efforts to address prisoner rape are in the early stages in South Africa. The DCS is developing initiatives focused on the link between prisoner rape, gangs, and HIV/AIDS. For example, in 2008, the DCS convened a day-long "Seminar on Offender Rape in Correctional Centres," bringing together senior corrections officials, nongovernmental organizations (including JDI [Just Detention International]), oversight officials, and academics to analyze the problem and to develop a response. At the invitation of the DCS, JDI has since provided a five-day 'master training' for corrections officials at Pollsmoor Prison—one of South Africa's most notorious detention facilities—in order to create a core group of staff who are equipped to address sexual abuse and the spread of HIV.

> *"HIV prevalence in South Africa is among the highest in the world, and the rate among prisoners is estimated to be more than double that of the general population."*

South Africa Has Taken Steps to Address Prison Rape

With the passage of the Sexual Offenses Amendment Act [Criminal Law (Sexual Offences and Related Matters) Amendment Act, 2007] in 2007, the South African Parliament adopted a gender neutral definition of rape. Previously, when the victim was a man, rape was prosecuted as 'indecent assault'—a much lesser offense. In a country where 98 percent of prisoners are men, this legislative change represents an important move toward ending impunity for prisoner rape. Commenting on the new law, former DCS commissioner Vernie Petersen stated, "[w]hereas previously such an act against a male was euphemistically described as sodomy or assault, this definition liberates us from the inaction that engulfed South African penal institutions."

South Africa has developed an important model for independent oversight of its prisons, which, if fully utilized, could help put an end to sexual abuse in detention. The Judicial Inspectorate of Prisons (JIOP), an independent monitoring body, employs more than 200 community-based ombudspersons—Independent Prison Visitors (IPVs)—who have access to all South African prisons, are able to speak confidentially with inmates, and can assist with requests ranging from facility transfers to access to medical care. JDI has conducted workshops on sexual violence for these ombudspersons in order to increase their capacity to detect instances of sexual abuse, secure assistance for survivors, and identify policies and practices that contribute to the problem. South Africa is expected to enhance further its prison oversight capacity through the U.N. [United Nations] Optional Protocol to the Convention Against Torture (OPCAT), a protocol the government has signed, but not yet ratified.

Prisons in Post-Soviet Russia Incubate a Plague

Merrill Goozner

Merrill Goozner has been an economics correspondent for the Chicago Tribune, a former journalism professor at New York University, and a former director of the Integrity in Science Project. He is the author of The $800 Million Pill: The Truth Behind the Cost of New Drugs. *In the following viewpoint, he explains that between 1991 and 2001, the collapse of the Soviet Union created unemployment and a crippled health care system, circumstances that contributed to a massive tuberculosis (TB) outbreak in Russian prisons. Today, thanks to efforts by international relief organizations, tuberculosis is controlled, but overcrowded conditions mean that the disease remains a danger.*

As you read, consider the following questions:

1. According to one estimate, between 1991 and 2001, how many cases of tuberculosis (TB) were there per 100,000 inmates in Russia's prisons?
2. By how much did the annual rate of new TB cases among the general population in Russia increase during the 1990s?
3. What is DOTS?

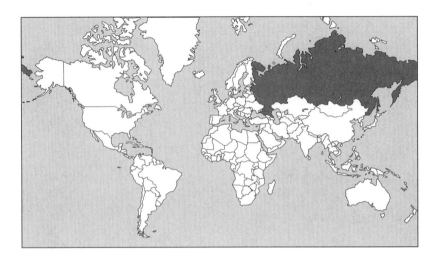

Prisoners in western Siberia who contract tuberculosis (TB) get sent to a forbidding complex in the heart of this provincial city. Armed guards with dogs patrol the nearby streets. Barbed wire covers the top of the outer walls. Iron bars clang shut when anyone enters. TB can keep you out of a remote Siberian prison camp, but it doesn't keep you out of jail.

Prison TB Becomes an Epidemic

And a decade ago, passing through this prison hospital's portals also posed a significant risk of premature death. Between 1991 and 2001 the incidence of TB in Russia's prisons reached a staggering 7,000 cases per 100,000 inmates, according to one estimate. Prisoners made up 25 percent of all new cases in the nation. In this oil-rich province the size of New Mexico with just over a million inhabitants, the prison TB rate reached the equivalent of 4,000 cases per 100,000 inmates, with nearly one of every 11 cases proving fatal.

The massive economic dislocation that accompanied the collapse of the Soviet Union turned Russia into an ideal breeding ground for a TB epidemic. Unemployment and alcoholism skyrocketed. Health and social services collapsed. As petty theft and violent crime soared, the prison population swelled to more than a million, with millions more moving in and out of incarceration. Many developed TB either because their immune systems, weakened by drugs, alcohol and poor nutrition, could no longer keep latent TB in check (an estimated one third of the world's population has latent TB) or they caught it from other prisoners.

Prisoners Spread the Disease to Others

The prisons in turn became an "epidemiological pump" for spreading the disease throughout the general population. Ex-prisoners, often with improperly treated TB that had mutated into the multidrug-resistant form of the disease, moved back into cramped apartment blocs where, during the long, cold Siberian winters, hallways and unventilated apartments provided ideal conditions for airborne transmission to unwary neighbors, friends and family members. The annual rate of new TB cases among the general population in Russia more than doubled in the 1990s to 88 cases per 100,000 inhabitants. In Siberia the rate soared to over 130 new cases per 100,000 souls. For a comparison, the U.S. had around 10 cases per 100,000 residents per year during the same period, and currently has about four cases per 100,000 annually.

Russia's post-communism prisons incubated the TB epidemic at the very time that the nation's health care system, including its network of specialized hospitals and clinics for treating TB, underwent its own collapse. Antibiotics, traditionally produced in the satellite republics, were in short supply as barter trade with those newly independent states ended and nothing took its place. Money for diagnostic tests and microscopes to analyze sputum samples dried up. The result was stop-and-go drug treatments for many TB patients, which generated in Russia's Siberian provinces some of the highest rates of multidrug-resistant TB (MDR-TB) in the world.

The World Health Organization (WHO) at first tried to combat the epidemic by pushing Russia to adopt its proved guidelines for treating the disease—DOTS, for directly observed therapy, short course. The regimen entails six to nine months of daily treatment with four oral antibiotics, directly observed by health professionals to ensure compliance. Health ministry officials in Moscow resisted, preferring to stick with the system inherited from Soviet days where doctors individualized treatment for each patient and relied on partial lung removal for hard-to-treat cases.

But bureaucratic intransigence wasn't the problem here. Local doctors were more than willing to buck the national establishment and adopt DOTS. But their pharmacies had run dry. "We even lacked first-line drugs," recalls Alexander Pushkarev, the physician in charge of the prison TB hospital.

"Russia's post-communism prisons incubated the TB epidemic at the very time that the nation's health care system . . . underwent its own collapse."

International Agencies Help Fight TB

That only began to change in the late 1990s when financier and philanthropist George Soros as well as international relief organizations—first Great Britain's Medical Emergency Relief International, or Merlin, and later the Boston-based Partners in Health (PIH)—began using this province as a testing ground for developing a comprehensive program to combat TB. Funders over the years have included Soros's Open Society Institute, the Bill and Melinda Gates Foundation, the Eli Lilly and Company Foundation and, since 2004, the Global Fund to Fight AIDS, Tuberculosis and Malaria, which gave the local health authorities a five-year, $10.7 million grant.

The strategy at first focused on bringing DOTS to Russia. But, starting in September 2000, the groups began taking a riskier and more expensive approach that had been developed by PIH in Peru. They encouraged local doctors, first in the

Tuberculosis Is Widespread in Uzbek Prisons

Independent rights activists say tuberculosis is particularly widespread among Uzbek prison inmates, and prisons are considered the epidemiological pump behind the high rate of tuberculosis in the country.

Uzbekistan's penal system is a closed realm. Officials provide no statistics on the size of the prison population, but some sources estimate it at up to 65,000. There are no reliable figures on the TB infection rate among convicts. . . .

"There have been several cases of prisoners being released when they were near death and dying at home a week or two after their release," [Surat] Ikramov, [chairman of the Center for Human Rights Initiatives in Tashkent] says.

Gulnoza Saidazimova, "Uzbekistan:
TB Among Prison Population Highlights Broader Risks,"
Radio Free Europe/Radio Liberty,
July 26, 2007. www.rferl.org.

prison system and then throughout the region, to aggressively treat all cases of MDR-TB, which can take as long as two years with anywhere from six to eight drugs. Its architects dubbed it DOTS-Plus.

The strategy was facilitated by the creation in the late 1990s of a drug procurement consortium dubbed the Green Light Committee, organized by the WHO, the U.S. Centers for Disease Control [CDC], several NGOs and pharmaceutical firms like Eli Lilly that still manufactured the rarely used antibiotics such as capreomycin and cycloserine needed to treat MDR-TB. Guaranteed purchase contracts and subsidies enabled countries like Russia to buy these second-line drugs at sharply reduced prices. "The cost went from $10,000 to $15,000 per patient to $3,000 to $4,000 per patient," says Peter Cegielski, the CDC's MDR-TB specialist, who joined the committee in 2000 and chaired it from 2004 to 2006.

Before taking a small group of foreign reporters and physicians on a tour of the 1000-bed prison hospital (currently only 60 percent filled with TB patients), director Pushkarev claimed the eight-year-old program had dramatically improved results. "In 1996 we had 60 patients die a year. But with the DOTS-Plus program, the death rate has gone way down. Since 2000, we've had zero deaths among new cases," he said.

"Although those conditions are a marked improvement from a decade ago . . . the opportunity for reinfection is ever present under such crowded conditions."

Crowded Conditions Remain a Problem

The hospital infrastructure had to be almost entirely rebuilt. Global Fund money helped to build an airtight closet for collecting sputum. The lab for analyzing and culturing the samples got new equipment. Whereas prisoners with susceptible TB were sent to live in barracks, those found to have MDR-TB were sent to an isolation ward in the hospital, where they lived six to eight in the room.

Although those conditions are a marked improvement from a decade ago (at least the MDR-TB patients are isolated from other prisoners), the opportunity for reinfection is ever present under such crowded conditions. "Russia just doesn't get it with infectious disease," says Michael Rich, a physician with PIH who splits his time between Siberia and Rwanda. "They have great doctors and a motivated staff. But putting four to five people in a room in winter with the windows closed? Infection control is still an issue here."

Australian Prisons Are Ill-Equipped to Deal with Women Prisoners

Federation of Community Legal Centres, (Vic) Inc.

Federation of Community Legal Centres, (Vic) Inc. is the peak body for over 50 community legal centres (CLCs) in Victoria, the second-most populous state in Australia. CLCs are independent community organisations that provide free legal services to the public and focus on helping clients who face economic and social disadvantage. Smart Justice was an Australian community campaign that aimed to widen the debate about Australia's justice system in the lead up to the Victorian state election on November 25, 2006. In the following viewpoint, the Federation reports that women's incarceration rates are rising rapidly in Australia. The Federation argues that women have special health needs and are often victims of abuse and drug addiction. Also, women need to maintain contact with their children and receive education and training. The prison system is not well-equipped to deal with these issues. Therefore, community-based punishments for women would be preferable.

As you read, consider the following questions:

1. What percentage of prisoners were women in 2005?

Federation of Community Legal Centres, (Vic) Inc., "Abused, Addicted, Mentally Ill. Is Prison the Best Place for Women Offenders?" www.SmartJustice.org.au, 2006. Reproduced by permission of the author.

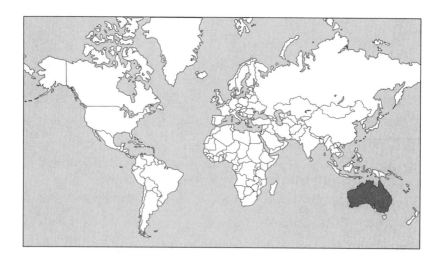

2. According to the Federation, what percentage of women entering prison in Victoria are estimated to have a drug or alcohol dependency?

3. According to the Federation, why are women prisoners often willing to submit to strip searches?

Women are going to jail in record numbers—a trend that has alarmed some experts and left the prison system struggling to cope.

Between 1998 and 2003, [the Australian state of] Victoria's female prison population increased by 84 percent, almost triple the growth of the male prison population over the same time. The increase was related to growth in: the use of remand [detention of subjects before trial], particularly for women with complex mental health and drug treatment needs; breaches of non-custodial orders [those with non-prison sentences violating the terms of their sentence]; violent and drug-related offending; [and] the number of women with no prior imprisonment or community corrections history who were sentenced to prison for a short term.

Imprisonment for Women Can Be Worse Than for Men

In a number of areas imprisonment can often be a much worse punishment for women. Women make up a much smaller percentage of the prison population but women prisoners are among the most vulnerable, unwell and disadvantaged groups in the corrections system.

Seven percent of prisoners were women in 2005, up from 4 percent in 1984. From 1991 to 1999 the number of women in prisons increased from 9.2 per 100,000 to 15.3 per 100,000—about a 66 percent increase—while the number of men in prisons over the same period rose only by 24 percent (194 to 240.5 per 100,000). Women are being jailed in record numbers and for longer sentences. In June 2000, 40 percent of women served sentences longer than 12 months. By June 2004, [that number had risen to] 59 percent.

> "Women prisoners are among the most vulnerable, unwell and disadvantaged groups in the corrections system."

Women in prison have a greater burden of disease and ill health than their male counterparts. Women are more likely to have chronic illnesses such as hepatitis and asthma and also experience more ill health symptoms.

Women's health care in prisons is an example of indirect discrimination against women—while women's health care needs are greater (for example, the requirement of health care that actively addresses reproductive health) women do not receive an increased level of care. Moreover, women in prison have less access to specialist services, more barriers to accessing tertiary health care [specialized care] and less availability of intensive mental health care than their male counterparts.

Despite the greater and more complex health needs of women in prison they are not provided with appropriate facilities. This discrimination is often justified because women prisoners are in such small numbers.

There is growing alarm about the lack of services for women prisoners in Victoria. Women in prison are 1.7 times more likely than men to have a mental illness—and 84.5% of women in prison had a mental disorder compared with 19.1% of women in the community. 51% of women surveyed reported having been diagnosed with a mental health illness prior to their incarceration.

Women Prisoners Suffer from Addiction and Abuse

Professor Paul Mullen, clinical director of the Victorian Institute of Forensic Mental Health, says much of the growth in the women's prison population stems from drug and public nuisance offences [prostitution]. The inadequacy of drug treatment facilities for women has been identified as a key problem area in the management of female prisoners in all Australian states. In Victoria, it has been estimated that 80% of women enter prison with a drug or alcohol dependency. 67% reported a connection between their drug and alcohol abuse and the offending behaviour. Two-thirds of first-time offenders reported drug abuse before their imprisonment, compared to 92% serving second or subsequent sentences.

It has been consistently documented that a large majority of women in prison have histories of physical and sexual abuse including abuse as children and intimate partner violence.

In a study of women prisoners, 77% reported a history of past abuse. *The Prisoner Health Survey* shows that in the 12 months prior to imprisonment alone, over 30 percent of all young women and 17 percent of older women had been physically hurt by their partner; around 10 percent had been raped by their partner.

Rates of Women in Prison for Selected Countries, 2006

Country	Rate of Women Incarcerated per 100,000 of Female Population
United States	123
Thailand	88
Russia	73
England and Wales	17
South Africa	14
France	6
India	3

TAKEN FROM: Christopher Hartney, "U.S. Rates of Incarceration: A Global Perspective," *National Council on Crime and Delinquency*, November 2006. www.nccd-crc.org.

More than half of a sample of women at the Dame Phyllis Frost Centre (DPFC) [a women's prison] reported being physically abused in childhood or adolescence, with 68 percent reporting emotional abuse and 44 percent reporting sexual abuse.

"A large majority of women in prison have histories of physical and sexual abuse including abuse as children and intimate partner violence."

Violence and abuse has significant and far-reaching health impacts beyond the immediate physical harm that women experience. It can lead to drug abuse, self-harm, depression, suicide attempts and reproductive health problems. Women in prison require services that actively address these issues. Breaking this cycle of abuse, violence, fear and crime through rehabilitation, support and treatment is in the interests of the community as a whole.

Women Need Education and Contact with Their Children

43% of female prisoners reported that at the time of imprisonment they were the carer of dependents—previous research has indicated that a high percentage of children of women in prison will also end up in prison. In addition, 44% of the women who were previously carers have no contact with those that they previously cared for.

Owing to the importance to women of maintaining contact with their families (especially their children) most female prisoners report being willing to submit to strip searches to maintain contact, despite the practice being state-sanctioned sexual assault.

Educational provision to women's prisons is of a poorer quantity, quality, variety and relevance than that offered in men's prisons.

"The provision of education and employment training is a key to keeping women out of prison. Programs at women's prisons are inadequate to address these issues."

67% of women prisoners were, at the time of their imprisonment, in an economic position to require some sort of government benefit. Of the women surveyed, 40% had not received a year 10 education, compulsory for the state.

The provision of education and employment training is a key to keeping women out of prison. Programs at women's prisons are inadequate to address these issues. In most prisons women must participate in either education, employment or other programs in order to be paid a wage, yet very few programs or education or employment options exist.

Instead of imprisoning more women, the government needs to invest in more effective alternatives to custody and crime diversion schemes. The best way to reduce women's offending is by tackling the causes—by improving education and employment training, [providing] mental health services, [and] tackling drug abuse and through community based punishments.

Juveniles in the United States Should Not Be Sent to Adult Prisons

J. Steven Smith

J. Steven Smith is a professor of justice education at Taylor University in Fort Wayne, Indiana. In the following viewpoint, Smith notes that in the United States in the late 1990s, adult prisons housed more than five thousand juveniles and adult jails detained more than nine thousand youths. About 40 percent were probably incarcerated for drug-related or nonviolent property offenses, rather than for violent crimes. Smith contends that law enforcement propaganda has caused fear by describing a nonexistent epidemic of juvenile crime, which has remained static at 20 percent of the overall crime rate since the 1980s. This fear has led to the imposition of adult prison terms as a means of deterring juvenile criminals. The frequently assigned shorter period of court supervision for juvenile cases, however, gives juvenile offenders the wrong impression that sentencing is easier, which leads to additional crimes. In addition, juveniles in adult prisons learn to commit new and more serious crimes. Smith asserts that courts should institute a restorative justice model aimed at making juvenile offenders provide restitution to their victims, schools should provide counselors and other social service professionals, and judges should have a range of sanctions to

J. Steven Smith, "Adult Prisons: No Place for Kids," *USA Today Magazine*, July 1, 2002. Copyright © 2002 Society for the Advancement of Education. Reproduced by permission.

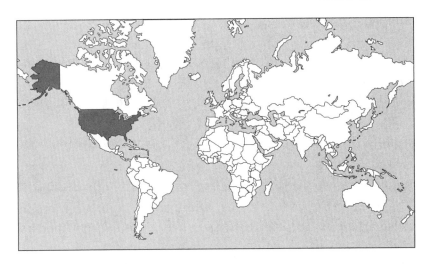

*use against unlawful juvenile acts, with incarceration in an
adult prison as a last resort for only the most extreme cases.*

As you read, consider the following questions:

1. What amendment to the Juvenile Justice and Delinquency Prevention Act of 1974 was passed?
2. What insight does the MacArthur Foundation Research
Network on Adolescent Development and Juvenile Justice give for why juveniles should not be tried and incarcerated as adults?
3. How much does it cost to keep a child in a adult prison,
according to Smith?

Several years ago, one of the news feature shows on television had an interviewer talking with a freckle-faced, red-
headed 12-year-old boy. The interview was taking place in a
maximum-security prison yard.

When asked what he had done to warrant being in the
prison, the youngster related how he had been spotted by local police as he drove a stolen car. After a high-speed chase, he
crashed into an interstate highway roadblock. Several state and
local law enforcement agencies and dozens of police cars were
involved.

The interviewer asked if the child was sorry for what he had done because it had resulted in a sentence to an adult maximum-security prison. The boy responded that he would do it again because it was the "greatest day" of his life!

"It was just like *Smokey and the Bandit* [a popular chase film]!" the boy effused. Clearly, he continued after a period of months to be caught up in the childish excitement of his criminal act. A mature sorrow for his actions and the resulting punishment were absent. Children are immature by definition.

This practice of locking up young people with adult criminals harkens back to the policies of the 1700s, when offenders, regardless of age, were thrown together in poorhouses and workhouses. The results were predictable. The young people got worse as a result of exposure to the more hardened criminals. It is hard to believe that, with the amount of scientific evidence we have generated over the last 100 years, political leaders still believe it is a good idea to lock misbehaving children up with adult criminals.

"While most of us would expect that youths in adult prisons were the most violent and dangerous juvenile offenders, the Department of Justice reported that 39% of the juveniles in adult prisons were sentenced for a nonviolent offense."

Today, there are thousands of young people living desperate lives locked away in adult prisons. Across the nation, the U.S. Department of Justice estimates there were about 5,500 juveniles being held in adult prisons in the late 1990s. There is little doubt that there are more than that now. Additionally, there are over 9,000 youths being held in the nation's adult jails.

While most of us would expect that youths in adult prisons were the most violent and dangerous juvenile offenders, the Department of Justice reported that 39% of the juveniles in adult prisons were sentenced for a nonviolent offense. The most serious charge for almost 40% of these young Americans was most likely a drug or nonviolent property offense. It is reasonable to propose that seriously violent youths should be held in adult facilities only if they are incapable of being effectively managed in a juvenile facility.

In 1980, Congress passed amendments to the Juvenile Justice and Delinquency Prevention Act of 1974. Chief among these amendments was a requirement to separate juveniles from adults in the nation's jails. This required local jails absolutely to prevent juveniles from seeing or hearing adult offenders. This provision was strictly enforced and required the restructuring of supervision for more than 6,000 juveniles in Indiana alone, for instance. This amendment is still on the books in spite of the ever-increasing use of adult prisons and jails for juvenile offenders.

Many juvenile justice experts believe that locking away youngsters in adult prisons is a response formed out of panic and fear. As William J. Chambliss states in *Power, Politics, and Crime*, "Panic over youth crime is as persistent in Western society as is worry about the stock market, but, like so many other alarms, it is based on political and law enforcement propaganda, not facts." In the late 1990s, another spate of law enforcement-driven propaganda about the "time bomb" of juvenile crime blossomed. That campaign was closely linked to the creation of anxiety over the state of the family in the U.S., where children were said to be growing up "fatherless, jobless, and godless," dependent on "welfare moms."

Elected officials realized that the public wanted something done about the "crime epidemic" that people believed was afflicting the nation. Rather than tell the public that there was not a crime wave, politicians responded with a great effort to "punish offenders back to righteousness." Not only has it been proven beyond any doubt that long prison terms do not reduce the crime rate, but elected officials failed to tell the public that they were safer than they had been since the 1960s. Juvenile crime—in fact, all crime—has been in decline over the last several years.

The percentage of crimes attributable to juveniles has remained stable at just under 20% since the 1980s. There is no scientific reason for a special effort directed at juvenile crime, but there certainly is political advantages to building up crime as a major social problem. "Although the number of juveniles arrested remained relatively stable over the 1990s, there has been an unending public diatribe about the increasing danger posed by juvenile crime," according to Albert J. Meehan in "The Organizational Career of a Statistic: Gang Statistics and the Politics of Policing Gangs," a 1998 report to the Office of Juvenile Justice and Delinquency Prevention.

The calls from elected officials and law enforcement agencies have been loud and clear. They argue that there is a "tidal wave of juvenile crime" at the edge of American cities and it is threatening to overwhelm communities unless there are tough new laws and penalties to dissuade juvenile offenders. Thus, they maintain, there is only one thing that officials see as a "real" deterrent to juvenile criminals, and that is the adult prison, which is almost universally viewed to be the most serious response available to legislators who are concerned about punishing crime.

In March, 2001, the *Pittsburgh Post-Gazette* reported on the "new era" that was begun in the mid-1990s. The politicians promised a tough new policy of cracking down on violent juvenile criminals. No more would "brutal teenagers be coddled" by juvenile courts, thereby encouraging additional misbehavior.

This idea is not supported by the literature on juvenile delinquency. A juvenile offender is typically placed under the supervision of the juvenile court until the age of majority (18–21, depending on the state). Adult courts that try juvenile offenders are often less likely to require intensive treatment and will often call for a much shorter period of court supervision. The juvenile offender looks at the shorter "sentence" from the adult court as a "free pass" to commit additional illegal acts.

Legislators even outlawed the traditional fact-finding role of the judge. The Building Blocks for Youth initiative reports that youths who are tried as adults are not being waived to adult court by the traditional judicial review of the particular facts. Instead, prosecutors or legislators are making 85% of these critical decisions. This practice does not allow a full airing of the facts in a juvenile case and therefore hurts the cause of justice. So, legislators sought not only to treat juveniles more harshly in adult court, but removed the traditional oversight protections of the courtroom judge.

According to the MacArthur [Foundation] Research Network on Adolescent Development and Juvenile Justice, "From a developmental perspective, many youths do not have the cognitive, emotional, and social maturity that they will have when they are adults. Moreover, considerable evidence has indicated higher prevalence of mental disorders among youths who come before the courts than among youths in general, including developmental delays, mental illnesses, and mental retardation."

It is not uncommon to see juveniles "showing tough" when they first arrive at any correctional institution, but when they do that at an adult maximum-security institution, it can have disastrous results. As Ronnie Greene and Geoff Dougherty reported in the *Miami Herald* on Sept. 7, 2001, "Florida's youngest prison inmates are also its most likely victims of reported assaults."

They indicated that juveniles locked up in adult male prisons are four times more likely than adults to report being assaulted, and 21 times more likely to be assaulted than teens held in one of Florida's secure juvenile facilities. They also pointed out the likelihood that one-half of these improperly placed juveniles will be assaulted while incarcerated.

Barbara White Stack of the *Pittsburgh Post-Gazette* (March 18, 2001) reported a similar failure of the "get tough on kids" program in Pennsylvania. She noted that these new get-tough laws have been described as being "both unfair and ineffective," increasing the probability a youth would "commit new crimes," and making youths "more likely to commit more serious new offenses."

"[Ronnie Greene and Geoff Dougherty] also pointed out the likelihood that one-half of these improperly placed juveniles will be assaulted while incarcerated."

The children who have been charged with "adult crimes" are among the most vulnerable youngsters in the nation. Of those charged as adults in Pennsylvania, "more than half had suffered abuse or neglect as children, and at least 40% were the children of criminals."

The new get-tough laws aimed at punishing juveniles have been implemented and found wanting on a number of fronts. First, these laws are unnecessary. Juvenile crime is decreasing, and youths continue to represent a small percentage of the crime rate. Almost half of the juveniles who are locked away in dangerous adult prisons committed a nonviolent crime, which could be effectively addressed by the juvenile courts. Second, these laws injure young people. Incarcerated youths run a great risk of being assaulted by adult inmates, and adult prisons become schools of crime for these youngsters.

Based on scientific research and common sense, there are many ideas that will address juvenile crime in a cost-effective fashion while maximizing community safety. There are dozens of organizations across the nation capable of assisting elected

Private Jails Bribe Judges in Pennsylvania

Last week [late February 2009] two judges in Pennsylvania were convicted of jailing some 2,000 children in exchange for bribes from private prison companies.

Mark Ciavarella and Michael Conahan sent children to jail for offenses so trivial that some of them weren't even crimes. A 15-year-old called Hillary Transue got three months for creating a spoof Web page ridiculing her school's assistant principal. Mr. Ciavarella . . . gave 14-year-old Jamie Quinn 11 months in prison for slapping a friend during an argument, after the friend slapped her. The judges were paid $2.6 million by companies belonging to the Mid-Atlantic Youth Services, Corp. for helping to fill its jails. This is what happens when public services are run for profit.

George Monbiot, "The Proceeds of Crime,"
Dissident Voice, *March 3, 2009.*
http://dissidentvoice.org.

officials in the development of more-reasonable responses to juvenile misbehavior. Some well-researched ideas that have been proposed by these groups include:

First and foremost, it is critical for society to move away from the current punishment-oriented philosophies towards a restorative justice model, which focuses on restoring everyone involved to his or her pre-crime state. Restoration of the victim clearly is first priority. This idea is particularly well-suited to property crimes and, since nonviolent property crimes comprise about 40% of all juvenile crimes, restoring victims would greatly reduce the number of youths incarcerated, while at the same time providing victims with restitution for their losses.

With regard to juvenile crime, communities need to develop and support intensive early childhood intervention programs to promote healthy families. In most communities, schools are the focal point for youths and their families. Accordingly, schools need to be the focus for prevention programs. Since youths show maladaptive signals early in their lives, it is important to assure that intervention is provided in the early grades. Elementary schools need to focus on providing counselors and social service personnel, rather than metal detectors and armed police officers, to stop the violence.

There must be a continuum of sanctions available to local judges, permitting a disposition that will best meet the needs of the juvenile, victim, and community. This continuum should range from fines and community service sanctions to restoration of the victim, probation, in-home detention, and electronic monitoring. Incarceration should be the last resort, and incarceration of a juvenile in an adult facility must be an extremely rare occurrence.

Communities would be well-served to reduce the agency "turf" issues that keep well-coordinated services from families that are in need. In many communities, there is little or no coordination among welfare, juvenile court, state corrections, and law enforcement officials. These agencies have to staff the youth and family service needs together so that a realistic plan can be developed and implemented.

"In many communities, there is little or no coordination among welfare, juvenile court, state corrections, and law enforcement officials. These agencies have to staff the youth and family service needs together so that a realistic plan can be developed and implemented."

These recommendations are not expensive options when we compare the price to implement them with the costs necessary to fortify our schools and the $30-50,000 per year we spend to keep a child in an adult prison.

Recently, the American Youth Policy Forum, the Child Welfare League of America, the Coalition for Juvenile Justice, the National Collaboration for Youth, the National Crime Prevention Council, the National League of Cities, and the National Urban League co-published *Less Hype, More Help: Reducing Juvenile Crime, What Works—and What Doesn't*. This major effort makes a number of well-reasoned proposals to reduce the juvenile crime rate, and their overall conclusions are certainly worthy of note:

- End overreliance on corrections and other out-of-home placements.

- Invest in research-based interventions for juvenile offenders, as well as research-based prevention.

- Measure results; find what works; and cut funds to what doesn't work.

- Engage community partners.

- Mobilize whole communities to study, plan, and implement comprehensive strategies for combating youth crime.

Periodical Bibliography

C. Farrell and
Investigator

"Judicial Caning in Singapore, Malaysia, and
Brunei," *Corpun*, October 2008.

Gregory Feifer

"Former Inmates Allege Russian 'Torture
Prisons,'" NPR, July 13, 2008.

Guy Hubbard

"UNICEF and Cameroon Work to Improve
Conditions for Female Prisoners," UNICEF,
April 14, 2008.

Immigration and
Refugee Board of
Canada

"Turkey: Prison Conditions and Treatment of
Prisoners in Civilian and F-Type Prisons, Including the Prevalence of Torture and the State
Response to It (2006–2007)," *Refworld*, June 7,
2007. www.unhcr.org.

Integrated Regional
Information Networks
(IRIN)

"Benin: Prison Conditions Violate Human
Rights," July 30, 2008. www.unhcr.org.

Integrated Regional
Information Networks
(IRIN)

"DRC: Mass Rape in Goma Prison," June 24,
2009. www.unhcr.org.

LICADHO

"Prison Conditions in Cambodia 2008: Women
in Prison," March 2009.

Tracy McNicoll

"Incarceration Nation: French Prisons Are Becoming an Embarrassment," *Newsweek*, August
2, 2008.

ROHR Zimbabwe

"Zimbabwe Prison Conditions Appalling. . . ."
April 28, 2009.

Sentencing and
Criminal Policy
Between Rechtsstaat &
Gottesstaat

"Women's Prison in Iran," April 11, 2007.
http://rezael.typepad.com.

Jonathan Steele

"Inmates Tell of Sexual Abuse and Beatings in
Iraq's Overcrowded Juvenile Prison System,"
Guardian, September 8, 2008.

GLOBALVIEWPOINTS

CHAPTER 4

I Political Prisoners

Iran Jailed a Prominent Journalist for Criticizing the Government

Golnaz Esfandiari

Golnaz Esfandiari was born in Iran and is a correspondent in Radio Free Europe/Radio Liberty's Central Newsroom. In this viewpoint, she reports on the imprisonment of Akbar Ganji, a journalist who criticized the Iranian government. The authorities demanded that he must recant his views before they would consider his release. Ganji has refused to recant and has undertaken a hunger strike to force his unconditional release. Esfandiari explains that human rights groups and Ganji's family fear he may die in prison.

As you read, consider the following questions:

1. During his hunger strike, on what was Akbar Ganji subsisting, according to reports?
2. What is the name of Ganji's two-part book?
3. On what charges was Ganji sentenced to ten years in prison in 2001?

Iran's most prominent jailed investigative journalist, Akbar Ganji, has been jailed for the last five years because of his critical articles and his investigation into the murders of po-

Golnaz Esfandiari, "Iran: Concern Grows over Fate of Jailed Journalist," *Radio Free Europe/Radio Liberty Online*, July 12, 2005. Copyright © 2009 RFE/RL, Inc. All rights reserved. Reprinted with the permission of *Radio Free Europe/Radio Liberty*, 1201 Connecticut Ave., N.W. Washington D.C. 20036. www.rferl.org.

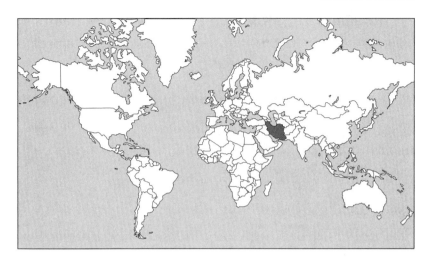

litical dissidents and intellectuals—murders in which, he says, top Iranian officials were involved. Now, Ganji's wife says that he has been on hunger strike for a month as he demands to be released unconditionally from prison. On 12 July [2005], a gathering is due to take place in Tehran in his support.

Ganji Maintains His Hunger Strike

Despite his poor health, Iran's top journalist Akbar Ganji is determined to continue his hunger strike until his unconditional freedom.

"[Investigative journalist Akbar] Ganji has criticized the authority of Iran's supreme leader and said that under the country's current governmental system real democracy cannot be achieved."

Ganji's wife Massoumeh Shafii was able to visit him on 11 July [2005]. She told RFE/RL [*Radio Free Europe/Radio Liberty*] that he believes a hunger strike is the only way to secure his freedom.

She also says Ganji has lost more than 20 kilograms [44 pounds] as a result of his hunger strike, but that his morale is good.

"He is still on a hunger strike. His weight is 55 kilos [121 pounds] now. He has lost a lot of weight during his hunger strike, he's without any force, the color of his face is yellow, and he tries very hard to speak normally," Shafii said. "His physical condition is not good, but he is in excellent spirits."

The journalist is reported to be subsisting on water and sugar cubes.

Ganji is known for his criticism of the Iranian establishment. He has said that his five years in jail, including several months in solitary confinement, has made his views even more radical.

In his two-part book titled *Manifesto of Republicanism*, Ganji has criticized the authority of Iran's supreme leader and said that under the country's current governmental system real democracy cannot be achieved.

The Iranian Government Wants Ganji to Recant

Ganji was temporarily released from jail at the end of May [2005] on medical grounds. He suffers from asthma and back pain. Prior to his temporary release, he had also been on a hunger strike to protest his detention conditions.

Several days after his release, he spoke with Radio Farda [a Persian language radio station supported by the United States] and called for a boycott of the 17 June [2005] Iranian presidential election.

"Those who are theoretically and practically committed to Iran's Constitution, if they go after reforming the current ruling establishment, maybe they are taking the right way," Ganji said at the time. "But if someone's main concern is democracy and establishing a democratic regime that is bound to human rights, then that person would not be willing to reform the establishment; his main issue would be how to move from an un-democratic regime to a democratic regime. And I've written in the first and second *Manifesto* that under the current regime I have no hope for any reform leading to a transition toward a democratic system."

On 11 June [2005], shortly after making this statement, Ganji was returned to prison.

"Iranian officials have told him that unless he changes his views, he will not be released even after his jail term is over."

Ganji was sentenced to 10 years in prison in 2001 on charges ranging from harming Iran's national security to spreading lies against the country's leaders. His sentence was later reduced to six years on appeal.

Ganji's wife told RFE/RL that Iranian officials have told him that unless he changes his views, he will not be released even after his jail term is over.

"Mr. Ganji says, 'Even after the few months left of my jail term would be over, [the authorities] will not free me because they have said it to me very clearly,'" Shafii said. "Even Trade Minister Mr. [Mohammad] Shariatmadari—who visited Ganji in jail two years ago—told him: 'the position of the establishment is that you should stay in jail until you [retract] what you have written in the *Manifesto*. You have to say that you were wrong.' [Therefore] Ganji considers his unconditional release as the only solution."

In a recent open letter written from jail and published on several Web sites, Ganji said he will not take back his words and he will not show remorse.

Akbar Ganji Is Released

Iran's most prominent political prisoner, Akbar Ganji, was released on the evening of 17 March 2006 after serving a six-year prison term. Even though he appeared aged and frail by a lengthy hunger strike, his release was celebrated as [a] sign of victory by dissidents and human rights activists. . . .

The change in his appearance after a long jail term . . . made him hard to recognise: He looked gaunt and unhealthy, and wore a long, heavy beard.

His persistence and bold views, which many shared but had not dared to articulate, had made him a respected figurehead of civil, non-violent resistance. . . .

Nazila Fathi, "Akbar Ganji's Moment,"
openDemocracy, July 4, 2006. www.opendemocracy.net.

Human Rights Advocates Call for Ganji's Release

There have been widespread calls for Ganji's release, including from Nobel Peace Prize Laureate Shirin Ebadi. In a June 30 [2005] interview with Radio Farda, Ebadi expressed concern over Ganji's health.

"'We are worried and there is nothing we can do,' [Ganji's wife Massoumeh] Shafii said. 'We are just witnessing how Akbar Ganji is fading out.'"

"Once more I would like to bring the worrying condition of Akbar [to] human rights groups," Ebadi said. "If no immediate action is taken he could [die].". . .

The EU, the United States, and several human rights groups have also called on Iran's judiciary to free Ganji.

Ganji's wife says she has written to many humanitarian organizations about her husband's condition.

"We are worried and there is nothing we can do," Shafii said. "We are just witnessing how Akbar Ganji is fading out. We've tried all the [channels] inside Iran but unfortunately there haven't been any results. We've been also following the case outside Iran, we've been sending letters to the European parliament, [EU foreign and security policy chief] Javier Solana, to the UN, to [UN Secretary-General] Kofi Annan. We've sent letters to all places we could and [brought their attention] to Mr. Ganji's case. There is international pressure but it's not clear when the Iranian officials will respond."

Today [July 12, 2005], a group of human rights activists, students and families of political prisoners have announced they will gather in front of Tehran's university to express their concern over Ganji's "critical" condition and to protest against the violation of his rights.

They say "if something unpleasant happens to Ganji, Iran's rulers will be held responsible."

China May Be Harvesting the Organs of Political Prisoners

David Matas

David Matas is the senior legal counsel of B'nai Brith Canada, a Jewish advocacy and community service organization, and he maintains a private practice in refugee, immigration, and human rights law. He is the co-author of the Report into Allegations of Organ Harvesting of Falun Gong Practitioners in China. *In this viewpoint, Matas argues that China has imprisoned large numbers of a peaceful sect known as Falun Gong. Based on evidence from his investigations, Matas maintains that China is harvesting these prisoners' organs for transplant operations, killing the prisoners in the process.*

As you read, consider the following questions:

1. According to David Matas, what two individuals initially made claims that organ harvesting was happening at Liaoning Hospital in Sujiatin, China?

2. How long are waiting times for organ transplants in China?

3. According to Matas, no law existed in China to prevent the selling of organs until what date?

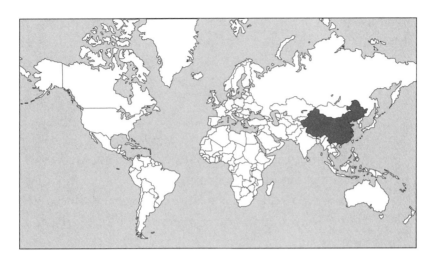

I s China harvesting organs of Falun Gong [a spiritual discipline founded in 1992] practitioners, killing them in the
process? A Japanese television news agency reporter and the
ex-wife of a surgeon in March made claims this was happening at Liaoning Hospital in Sujiatin, China. Are those claims
true?

> *"The Communist Party of China, for no apparent reason
> other than totalitarian paranoia, sees Falun Gong as an
> ideological threat to its existence."*

Falun Gong Members Are Persecuted

The Coalition to Investigate the Persecution of Falun Gong in
China, an organization headquartered in Washington, D.C., in
May [2006] asked former Minister of State for Asia and the
Pacific David Kilgour and me to investigate these claims. We
released a report in July [2006] which came to the conclusion,
to our regret and horror, that the claims were indeed true.

The repressive and secretive nature of Chinese governance
made it difficult for us to assess the claims. We were not allowed entry to China, though we tried. Organ harvesting is

not done in public. If the claims are true, the participants are either victims who are killed and their bodies cremated or perpetrators who are guilty of crimes against humanity and unlikely to confess.

We examined every avenue of proof and disproof available to us, eighteen in all. They were:

- The Communist Party of China, for no apparent reason other than totalitarian paranoia, sees Falun Gong as an ideological threat to its existence. Yet, objectively, Falun Gong is just a set of exercises with a spiritual component.

- The threat the Communist Party perceives in the Falun Gong community has led to a policy of persecution. Persecution of the Falun Gong in China is officially decided and decreed.

- Falun Gong practitioners are victims of extreme vilification. The official Chinese position on Falun Gong is that it is "an evil cult."

- Falun Gong practitioners have been arrested in huge numbers. They are detained without trial or charge until they renounce Falun Gong beliefs.

- Falun Gong practitioners are victims of systematic torture and ill-treatment. While the claims of organ harvesting of Falun Gong practitioners have been met with doubt, there is no doubt about this torture.

- Many Falun Gong practitioners have formally disappeared; they are the subject of formal disappearance complaints by family members. Many more practitioners, in an attempt to protect their families and communities, have not identified themselves once arrested. These unidentified are a particularly vulnerable population.

- Traditional sources of transplants—executed prisoners, donors, the brain dead—come nowhere near to accounting for the total number of transplants in China. The only other identified source which can explain the skyrocketing transplant numbers is Falun Gong practitioners.

- Falun Gong practitioners in prison are systematically blood tested and physically examined. Yet, because they are also systematically tortured, this testing can not be motivated by concerns over their health.

- In a few cases, between death and cremation, family members of Falun Gong practitioners were able to see the mutilated corpses of their loved ones. Organs had been removed.

- We interviewed the Japanese journalist and the ex-wife of the surgeon from Sujiatin. Their testimony was credible to us. In order to be cautious, we relied on this testimony only when it was independently corroborated.

- We had callers phoning hospitals throughout China posing as family members of persons who needed organ transplants. In a wide variety of locations, those who were called asserted that Falun Gong practitioners (reputedly healthy because of their exercise regime) were the source of the available organs. We have recordings and telephone bills for these calls.

- Waiting times for organ transplants in China are incredibly short, a matter of days. Everywhere else in the world, waiting times are measured in years.

- Chinese hospital Web sites host incriminating information advertising organs of all sorts on short notice.

- A Falun Gong practitioner who had been in prison in China told us that her Chinese jailers lost interest in her once they found out that her organs had been damaged.

- China is a systematic human rights violator. The overall pattern of violations makes it harder to dismiss any one claimed violation.

- There is huge money to be made in China from transplants. Prices charged to foreigners, also available on a Web site, range from US$30,000 for corneas to US$180,000 for a liver and kidney combination.

- Corruption in China is a major problem. The huge money to be made from transplants, the lack of state controls over corruption and the marginalization of the Falun Gong are a deadly trio.

- Until July 1 of this year [2006], [there] was no law in China preventing the selling of organs and no law requiring consent for organ harvesting. China has a poor history of implementing laws designed to ensure respect for human rights.

"There is huge money to be made in China from transplants. Prices charged to foreigners, also available on a Web site, range from US$30,000 for corneas to US$180,000 for a liver and kidney combination."

Organ Harvesting Must Stop

It is easy to take each element in isolation, and say that this element or that does not prove the claim. But it is their combination which led us to the chilling conclusion to which we came.

We are reinforced in our conclusions by the feeble response of the Government of China. Despite all their resources

Organ Transplants at the Orient Organ Transplant Centre in Tianjin City

Organ transplant operations at a single facility increased exponentially, suggesting a new source of donors, possibly Falun Gong prisoners. As a comparison, in all of Canada there were only 1,773 organ transplants in 2004.

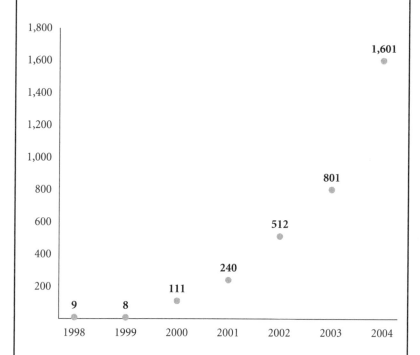

TAKEN FROM: David Matas and David Kilgour, *Bloody Harvest: Revised Report into Allegations of Organ Harvesting of Falun Gong Practitioners in China*, January 31, 2007. http://organharvestinvestigation.net.

and inside knowledge, they have not provided any information to counter our report. Instead, they have attacked us personally and, more worrisome, attacked the Falun Gong with the very sort of verbal abuse which we have identified as one of the reasons we believe these atrocities are occurring.

Our report has seventeen different recommendations. Virtually no precaution one can imagine to prevent the harvesting of organs of Falun Gong practitioners in China is currently being taken. All these precautions should be put in place.

But there is one basic recommendation we make which must be implemented immediately. Organ harvesting of Falun Gong practitioners in China must stop.

In China, Identifying Political Prisoners Can Facilitate Their Release

Andreas Lorenz

Andreas Lorenz is a reporter and writer for German news outlet Der Spiegel. In the following viewpoint, he reports on the work of John Kamm, a former American businessman who compiles lists of China's numerous political and religious prisoners. These lists and Kamm's personal contacts in China have been instrumental in obtaining the release of many individuals.

As you read, consider the following questions:

1. What sort of company did John Kamm work for in his past life?
2. Cai Zhuohua was sentenced to prison for three years for doing what?
3. What is the name of the organization Kamm founded in San Francisco?

In his past life, John Kamm was a broker for an American chemical company. The 55-year-old was also the respected president of the American Chamber of Commerce in Hong

Andreas Lorenz, "Making the Disappeared Re-Appear," translated by Christopher Sultan, *Der Spiegel*, March 6, 2006. Copyright © *Der Spiegel* 10/2006. All rights reserved. Reproduced by permission.

Kong, drove a company car and lived in a villa complete with servants. But all of that proved too upper middle class for Kamm, too materialistic—and he went looking for a new challenge.

It didn't take him long to find one.

Looking for Prisoners in China

Kamm has spent the last 16 years sifting through dreary columns of statistics, studying professional journals and perusing publicly accessible court documents—all on the search for religious and political prisoners in China. He and his colleagues have been remarkably successful. In a search funded almost completely by the charity of others, they have uncovered some 5,000 such prisoners.

Only recently, in fact, he discovered the names of a handful of dissidents in the state of Xinjiang who had dared to question Chinese supremacy in the predominantly Muslim region. They had become part of a large group of missing in a country that officially has no political prisoners. Some are the opponents of the Communist Party; others are members of banned religious groups and trade unionists—nothing but common criminals in the eyes of the establishment. And they are sentenced for crimes such as "incitement," "endangering the public order" or "endangering national security."

"This is part of daily life in China," says Kamm. It's also part of daily life that prison guards have the power to prolong a prisoner's sentence if they believe he or she is refusing to show the appropriate amount of remorse.

Kamm's Personal Contacts Aid in the Release of Prisoners

The fact that China's treatment of its dissidents reaches the light of day at all is thanks to another aspect of the Chinese system. The political police and the courts have an interest in local papers or professional journals reporting on the delinquents and their offences. Hunting down "enemies of the state" is both good for prosecutors' careers and meant to deter imitators.

Kamm, though, isn't just interested in discovering new cases. He heads off to China whenever new cases come to his attention and tries to leverage his numerous contacts with diplomats, prosecutors and police officials into help for the prisoners. Kamm's engaging persona and profound knowledge of life in the country have helped him develop a positive reputation within official China and he is regularly received at the Chinese foreign ministry. There, he hands over his lists of political prisoners—prisoners who, in Kamm's opinion, do not warrant further imprisonment.

His most recent list includes Zhao Yan, an assistant in the Beijing bureau of the *New York Times*. Yan has been held by the police without trial for almost a year and a half. Then there is Cai Zhuohua, a Protestant minister sentenced to three years in prison in 2005 for distributing Bibles. Four hundred political prisoners have been released early in the past two years—partly because their names were on Kamm's lists.

On a recent Thursday evening in Beijing, Kamm, a gray-haired man who looks older than his years, stands in front of foreign correspondents and talks about the fruits of his efforts. His diabetes has taken a toll—in addition to losing 10 kilograms (about 22 pounds) in the last few months, he has lost teeth and his new dentures are causing problems. But little can dampen his enthusiasm. "Prisoner lists most certainly have an impact," says Kamm.

"Four hundred political prisoners have been released early in the past two years—partly because their names were on Kamm's lists."

His success, of course, depends heavily on the whims of government officials and on the overall political climate. If a state visit by the American president is in the works, or if a high-ranking Beijing politician is on his way to Washington, the chances are good that the Chinese will release a few prisoners early. And even for those prisoners who are not released, having their names on Kamm's list is an advantage. It can mean receiving better treatment from guards, or perhaps an extra blanket, or being examined by a doctor and maybe even being allowed to receive visits from a relative.

China Holds Thousands of Political Prisoners

Kamm estimates that about 10,000 political prisoners are currently locked away in Chinese prisons. Some 30,000 police officers in addition to the national security agency routinely hunt down people who put up protest posters, plan demonstrations, write letters critical of the government, publish unwanted poems or organize democratic parties and workers' rights groups. Approximately 30,000 more officers monitor the Internet to find bloggers and seditious Web sites.

Those who are caught end up either in prison or in China's maze of state-run farms. Other destinations include psychiatric hospitals, re-education camps, or work camps operated by myriad different government agencies.

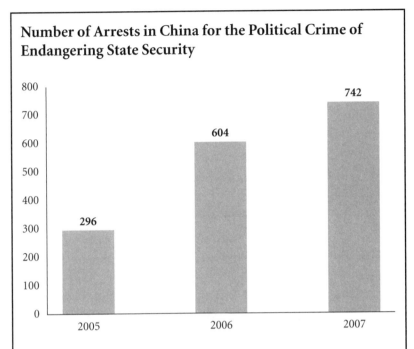

Number of Arrests in China for the Political Crime of Endangering State Security

TAKEN FROM: Dui Hua website, "Statistics Show Chinese Political Arrests Rose Again in 2007," March 16, 2008; "New Statistics Point to Dramatic Increase in Chinese Political Arrests in 2006," November 27, 2007. www.duihua.org.

Kamm's transformation into a human rights activist began when, during his days as a businessman, he worked as a lobbyist for Beijing in Hong Kong. Shortly after the Tiananmen Square massacre [in which the Chinese military attacked demonstrators] on June 4, 1989, he called upon Washington—in his position as president of the American Chamber of Commerce—to retain most-favored nation status for China to continue promoting trade with the country despite what had happened.

During a meal with a high-ranking Chinese official, he suddenly hit upon the idea of asking for something in return. He asked for the release of a student who had just been arrested. That was the beginning.

Kamm's outrageous demand quickly put a damper on the mood at the dinner. Nevertheless, the young man was released a few weeks later, and Kamm discovered that he had found his calling. Soon he was no longer able to reconcile business and his conscience, and so he founded the San Francisco-based Dui Hua Foundation, providing new hope for thousands of prisoners. Dui Hua means "dialogue" in Chinese.

"Kamm estimates that about 10,000 political prisoners are currently locked away in Chinese prisons."

Kamm relishes talking about his highest-profile case, that of Tibetan monk Tanak Jigme Sangpo, whose release he negotiated "for medical reasons" after Sangpo had spent 40 years in the notorious Drapchi Prison in Lhasa. Sangpo, a follower of the Dalai Lama [a major Tibetan Buddhist religious leader]—a man hated in Beijing—has been repeatedly jailed since 1965. Officials told Kamm that Sangpo no longer wanted to be released. But then Kamm was permitted to travel to Lhasa, and Sangpo was finally released—at 76. Today he lives in a monastery in Switzerland.

In Cuba, There Are Fewer Political Prisoners but More Arbitrary Arrests

Dalia Acosta

Dalia Acosta is a journalist and the Inter Press Service (IPS) correspondent in Havana, Cuba. In the following viewpoint, she reports that the number of political prisoners in Cuba has been steadily decreasing over the past few years. On the other hand, arbitrary detentions for short periods have increased. In either case, Cuba continues to repress political dissent. The government claims this repression is necessary if the country is to defend itself against the United States, which it says foments internal rebellion. Still, Cuba has made some moves toward less repression including encouraging debate on certain issues and promising to sign human rights conventions.

As you read, consider the following questions:

1. Who does the Cuban government accuse of financing the Cuban Commission for Human Rights and National Reconciliation (CCDHRN)
2. According to the December 31, 2007, CCDHRN report, how many political prisoners were there in Cuba at that time?

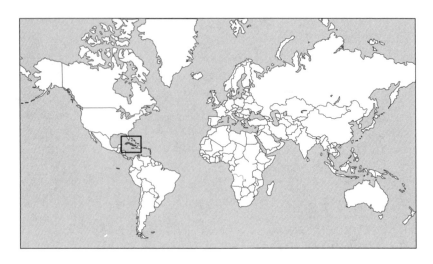

3. According to Acosta, what was the estimated prison population of Cuba as of January 2008?

The number of political prisoners in Cuba fell last year, but arbitrary detentions increased, according to a report released Wednesday by the Cuban Commission for Human Rights and National Reconciliation (CCDHRN).

At least 325 people were arbitrarily arrested—most of them were held by the authorities for some hours or a few days. Those apprehended "for trying to exercise certain civil and political rights" were released without charge, said CCDHRN, which has worked illegally in the country since 1987, but is tolerated by the authorities.

Cuba Blames the United States for Repressive Policies

"Our day-to-day observation leads us to think that the style of political repression has changed. The long prison terms handed down years ago have given way to short periods of detention," Elizardo Sánchez, a human rights observer and head of CCDHRN, told IPS [Inter Press Service].

"The current situation could continue in the short term, unless there are unforeseen changes in government policy," the activist said.

Manuel Cuesta Morúa, spokesman for the Arco Progresista dissident coalition, said that such "warnings" from the authorities are on the increase. "The limit still appears to be the street. The authorities are determined not to allow any public demonstration that might get out of hand," he told IPS.

According to the CCDHRN report, the interim government—in power since the announcement of President Fidel Castro's illness on Jul. 31, 2006—"has done nothing to change the dire situation of civil, political and economic rights that has existed in Cuba for more than four decades."

"'The style of political repression has changed. . . . The long prison terms handed down years ago have given way to short periods of detention.'"

The Cuban government, for its part, does not recognise the legitimacy of this kind of report, nor of organisations like CCDHRN, which the authorities say have no real influence in the country and only exist because they are promoted and financed by the United States government.

When it speaks on human rights, the Cuban government stresses the social achievements of the country and the benefits its 11.2 million people enjoy in terms of education, health and employment, guaranteed by the state.

The lack of other rights are officially attributed to the country's need to defend itself from the U.S.—which uses its U.S. Interests Section in Havana to promote internal rebellions—and has publicly declared its support for a change of government and an end to socialism on this island.

The U.S. has maintained an economic embargo against the island for over 40 years.

Journalists Are Jailed in Cuba

Reporters Without Borders points out that the Cuban government, for all its denials . . . continues to hold 23 journalists solely because of their dissident views and still refuses to permit an independent press.

The press freedom organization hopes that mediation by other Latin American countries and by Spain, and the new US administration's declared readiness to hold a dialogue could open the way to the release of the imprisoned journalists.

Reporters Without Borders,
"World Spotlight on Cuba's Repression,"
Panama News, *February 8, 2009.*
www.thepanamanews.com.

Cuba Makes Some Moves to Ease Repression

However, a public debate of the current problems troubling Cuban society—a debate stimulated in 2007 by the government itself—has brought up some issues that have been part of the dissident agenda, and are now being raised by broad sectors of the population.

Among the proposals being debated are the right to freely enter and leave the country, elimination of the present dual currency, extension of cooperative ownership to certain services, and access by Cubans to tourist hotels, from which they were banned 15 years ago.

The CCDHRN report was distributed to the press Wednesday. It includes a partial list of political and sociopolitical prisoners which the organization publishes every six months, based on information from relatives.

On Dec. 31 [2007] there were 234 political prisoners, 12 fewer than the number reported in mid-2007. The report considers this to be of minimal significance, but it is part of a clear trend. CCDHRN reported 333 documented political prisoners at the end of 2005, and 283 at the end of 2006.

Only 72 out of the 234 listed are accepted as prisoners of conscience by human rights watchdog Amnesty International (AI). Of these, 59 are serving sentences in maximum security jails, and 13 have been granted conditional release for health reasons.

According to CCDHRN, "If the government were to apply, without discrimination on ideological grounds, the provisions of Article 58, sections 1 and 2 of the current criminal code which establish the right to conditional release, nearly a hundred political prisoners could be freed from prison immediately."

The general prison population, estimated at 80,000 in the absence of official figures, could also be reduced by applying this provision. "Every time we see someone convicted of 'dangerousness' we know they are technically innocent because they have committed no crime," Sánchez said.

"Dangerousness" means someone is suspected to have the potential to commit a crime. It is a category that covers thousands of men and women who have been arrested.

"Every time we see someone convicted of "dangerousness" we know they are technically innocent because they have committed no crime."

The report says the government's recent announcement that it will sign the U.N. International Covenant on Civil and Political Rights (ICCPR) and [the U.N. International Covenant] on Economic, Social and Cultural Rights (ICESCR) is "positive, if Cuba is willing to respect the letter and the spirit of both pacts."

The decision means Cuba will open its doors to regular monitoring by the newly created U.N. Human Rights Council from 2009.

According to the CCDHRN report, instead of "signing more commitments," the government should respect the laws already in force in the country, and make headway by "reform[ing] laws that criminalise the exercise of elementary civil, political, economic and cultural rights."

Political Protestors in Papua Should Not Be Imprisoned

Human Rights Watch

Human Rights Watch (HRW) is an international nongovernmental organization that researches and advocates for human rights worldwide. In the following viewpoint, HRW reports that inhabitants of Papua, a remote part of Indonesia, are often imprisoned when they peacefully raise pro-independence flags or speak out in favor of independence. Such imprisonment violates international treaties that Indonesia signed in 2006. HRW asserts that to fulfill its obligations and to secure its place as a rights-respecting member of the international community, Indonesia should release all political prisoners and repeal laws restricting freedom of expression.

As you read, consider the following questions:

1. Why was December 1 designated a "national day" by Papuan nationalists?
2. According to Human Rights Watch (HRW), how many people were arrested in Papua for peaceful independence activities in 2002?
3. What are the two human rights treaties that Indonesia acceded to in 2006?

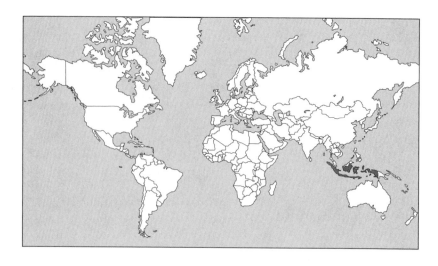

Papua, at the far eastern end of the Indonesian archipelago, is one of the most remote places in the country. This isolation, compounded by government imposed restrictions on access to the two provinces which make up Papua ("Papua" and "West Irian Jaya"), has contributed to a dearth of information on the human rights situation there. With international attention focused on the peace process [following a war between the Indonesian government and the Free Aceh Movement in 2003–2004] and post-tsunami reconstruction [after the Indian Ocean earthquake of 2004] in the province in Aceh, relatively little is known about recent human rights developments in Papua.

The Struggle in Papua Has Been Ignored

One consequence of Papua's remoteness has been that a series of criminal convictions in recent years of peaceful political activists has not attracted the attention it deserves. A low-level armed separatist insurgency in the province has resulted in a large military presence and a climate of mutual suspicion and fear. All too often Papuans not involved in the armed insurgency are caught up in anti-separatist sweeps or arrested as troublemakers for peacefully expressing their political views, a right protected by basic international free speech guarantees.

Pro-independence activists are frequently targeted for arrest. December 1 has been designated a "national day" by Papuan nationalists, commemorating the day in 1961 when a group of Papuans, promised independence by then-colonial ruler Holland, first raised the Papuan national flag, the *Bintang Kejora* (Morning Star) flag. Every year people mark this event by again raising, or attempting to raise, the flag. Most years these attempts end in clashes with local security forces intent on stopping what they see as treasonous activities against the Republic of Indonesia. They have almost always ended in arrests, and sometimes trials and convictions, often for the peaceful expression of political dissent. At other times activists are arrested merely for publicly expressing support for Papuan independence, or for attending peaceful meetings to talk about self-determination for Papua.

Human Rights Watch takes no position on Papuan claims to self-determination, but it supports the right of all individuals including independence supporters to express their political views peacefully without fear of arrest or other forms of reprisal. To the extent individuals are arrested and imprisoned for peaceful participation in symbolic flag-raising ceremonies, such treatment constitutes arbitrary arrest and detention in violation of international standards.

Indonesia Criminalizes Peaceful Dissent

Indonesian authorities commonly use two sets of criminal laws against activists in Papua. The first is the colonial era "hate sowing" (*Haatzai Artikelen*) articles of Indonesia's Criminal Code, which criminalize "public expression of feelings of hostility, hatred or contempt toward the government" and prohibit "the expression of such feelings or views through the public media." The articles authorize prison terms of up to seven years for violations.

The other criminal law provision most often used is one outlawing *"makar,"* which translates into English as rebellion. This is often used against persons arrested for their alleged participation in, or support for, separatism. The crime of *makar* is listed in Indonesia's criminal code in a section entitled "Crimes Against the Security of the State" (*Kejahatan Terhadap Keamanan Negara*). The articles authorize prison terms up to twenty years for the offences.

In May 2005, Filep Karma and Yusak Pakage, independence supporters . . . , were sentenced to 15- and 10-year prison sentences for organizing peaceful celebrations and flying the Morning Star flag in the provincial capital of Jayapura on December 1, 2004. They were charged and convicted both of spreading hatred and of rebellion. In an act of defiance, on December 1, 2005, Filep Karma managed to climb from his cell onto the roof of the prison and once again fly the Morning Star flag. Linus Hiluka, a thirty-four-year-old farmer . . . , is currently serving a 20-year jail term. His crime was his association with an organization called the Baliem Papua Panel, deemed a separatist organization by Indonesian authorities.

"There has been a long history of suppression of peaceful activism in Papua. Nonviolent flag raisers and protestors against Indonesian rule have been arrested, sometimes ill-treated, and convicted."

These convictions are not an aberration. They reflect government policy.

There has been a long history of suppression of peaceful activism in Papua. Nonviolent flag raisers and protestors against Indonesian rule have been arrested, sometimes ill-treated, and convicted for peacefully expressing their discontent through flag raising or other activities. In 2002 alone, forty-two people were arrested in Papua for peaceful independence activities. Over the last few years through a variety of announcements, the governor of Papua, the military commander, and the president of the High Court have also instructed people in Papua not to celebrate December 1. In 2004 the Papuan provincial chief of police, Inspector General Dodi Sumatyawan, stated that "the anniversary celebration is unlawful and parties who commemorate it will be severely punished."

"Peaceful campaigning for self-determination is a right protected by several human rights treaties . . . which Indonesia acceded to in February 2006."

In December 2005 TAPOL, the Indonesia Human Rights Campaign, a UK-based human rights organization, uncovered a confidential directive issued on November 10, 2005, by Chief of Police of Papua D.S. Sumantyawan. The directive instructed that anyone engaged in activities on a number of commemorative occasions in November and December would be liable to be charged under Indonesia's anti-subversion law. The terms of the directive make clear that this would encompass even those engaged in peaceful celebrations, which should be protected by the law. One of the dates highlighted by the police chief was December 1. Section Six of the November 10 directive orders police chiefs to:

Uphold the law in a clear and professional manner against all violations of the law that occur, in particular flying the Morning Star flag or the 14-point star flag, to arrest and detain those involved and confiscate evidence of flags, to be processed in accordance with the law, to face charges of subversion [*makar*] in a court of law.

The directive, which was sent in a telegram to all police commands in the territory, said that it had been sent within the framework of an operation called Mambruk II 2005.

> ## Selected Comparative Statistics: Indonesia as a whole versus Papua, 2007
>
> | | Indonesia | Papua |
> |---|---|---|
> | Poverty rate | 16.6% | 40.8% |
> | Children enrolled in primary school | 94.7% | 78% |
> | Life expectancy for women | 72.1 years | 50.3 years |
>
> TAKEN FROM: *Progressio*, "Millenium Development Goals in Papua," n.d. [c. 2008]. www.progressio.org.uk.

International Law Protects Peaceful Protest

Indonesian law distinguishes between cultural symbols used to express Papuan identity and symbols understood as a symbol of sovereignty. International law knows no such distinction. While the Papua Special Autonomy Law, passed in 2001, explicitly allows symbols of Papuan identity such as a flag or song, courts have treated the raising of flags associated with pro-independence sentiment as a symbol of sovereignty and, as such, a banned form of expression.

Peaceful campaigning for self-determination is a right protected by several human rights treaties, including the International Covenant on Civil and Political Rights (ICCPR) and the International Covenant on Economic, Social, and Cultural Rights (ICESCR), both of which Indonesia acceded to in February 2006. Human Rights Watch therefore considers individuals arrested, prosecuted, and imprisoned for peacefully expressing support for independence—whether through flag, song, or other means—as political prisoners. We know of at least eighteen such individuals in Papua. . . .

Freedom of expression is a basic right and often acts as an enabler of other rights. Conversely, where freedom of expression is not respected, other rights are rarely secure. In Papua, related human rights concerns include restrictions on freedom of assembly, arbitrary detention, and violation of the prohibition on inhuman and degrading treatment and torture. Until there is increased access to the province for foreign correspondents, diplomats, and independent monitors, including international human rights organizations, it will be impossible to reach clear conclusions about the state of human rights in the province. What is known, however, is cause for serious, ongoing concern.

In 2006 Indonesia succeeded in securing membership of both the UN Human Rights Council and the UN Security Council. In 2006, as already noted, Indonesia also acceded to the ICCPR and the ICESCR. These are signs that Indonesia wants to be accepted as a rights-respecting member of the international community. While Indonesia is certainly in a transition period, the repression detailed in this report shows that there is still much to be done in institutionalizing meaningful protections for basic human rights in the country: That flag raisers, or others peacefully campaigning for Papuan independence, should be imprisoned for their activities is indicative of how far Indonesia still has to go on its journey to become a fully rights-respecting and democratic nation. There is a clear gap between Indonesia's international commitments and rhetoric and the reality on the ground.

"Freedom of expression is a basic right and often acts as an enabler of other rights. Conversely, where freedom of expression is not respected, other rights are rarely secure."

The cases of Filep Karma and Yusak Pakage exemplify how real the gap is. If Filep Karma serves his full sentence it will be 2020 before he is released and he will be 61 years old. He will have spent the majority of his adult life in prison. His crime was nothing more than the expression of an opinion, the expression of a belief. He should not be in a cell for that.

Indonesia Should End Repression

Human Rights Watch urges the Indonesian government and parliament to:

- Immediately and unconditionally release all persons detained or imprisoned for the peaceful expression of their political views, including raising the Morning Star flag;

- Drop any outstanding charges against individuals awaiting trial for their peaceful political activities and make a public commitment to ensure no further arrests of individuals engaged in the peaceful expression of their beliefs;

- Repeal articles 154, 155, and 156 of the KUHP (Kitab Undang-Undang Hukum Pidana, Indonesian Criminal Code) criminalizing "public expression of feelings of hostility, hatred or contempt toward the government" and prohibiting "the expression of such feelings or views through the public media," and articles 106, 107, and 108 on treason. Make a public commitment not to undertake any further prosecutions using these laws; and

- End all arbitrary restrictions on access to Papua for journalists, diplomats and human rights organizations.

Periodical Bibliography

Amnesty International	"Ethiopia: Government Must Reveal Fate of Political Prisoners," May 5, 2009.
Amnesty International	"Hu Jia Jailed for Three and a Half Years," April 4, 2008.
Asian Human Rights Commission	"Indonesia: Torture and Maltreatment of Political Prisoners in Papua," February 16, 2009. www.ahrchk.net.
Cuban Democratic Directorate	"Cuban Activist at UN Condemns Systematic Torture, Seeks Support for Political Prisoners," *Directorio Democrático Cubano*, July 25, 2008. www.directorio.org.
Economist	"Out of Jail; Cuba's Political Prisoners," September 1, 2007.
Foreign Policy	"The List: Political Prisoners to Watch," September 2006. www.foreignpolicy.com.
Patricia Grogg	"Death Penalty-Cuba: Sentences Commuted but Treatment Still Harsh," IPS, 2008.
Blaine Harden	"Escapee Tells of Horrors in North Korean Prison Camp," *Washington Post*, December 11, 2008.
Human Rights Watch	"Burma: Free Aung San Suu Kyi," May 14, 2009.
Human Rights Watch	"Iran: Stop 'Framing' Government Critics," July 21, 2009.
Patrick Martin	"Washington's 'Democracy' in Iraq Hangs 13 Political Prisoners," *World Socialist*, March 11, 2006.
Maura Moynihan	"Prison, Torture for No Crime," Radio Free Asia, November 26, 2008.
The Other Russia	"Activists Urge Medvedev to Free Political Prisoners," May 23, 2008. www.theotherrussia.org.

For Further Discussion

Chapter 1

1. In Viewpoint 1-1, the Council of Europe provides four main justifications for imprisonment. Which of these justifications align with the views expressed by CIVITAS: The Institute for the Study of Civil Society in Viewpoint 1-4?

2. Viewpoint 1-2 by the Catholic Bishops of New Zealand and Viewpoint 1-3 by Louis Nevaer discuss Catholic attitudes toward imprisonment. Based on these discussions, does Catholic teaching seem to favor or oppose harsh punishments? Explain why using evidence from both viewpoints.

Chapter 2

1. In Viewpoint 2-2, Ipshita Sengupta notes, "When it comes to life imprisonment, there are no set, fully developed international standards." What differences are there between the application of life imprisonment in India, as Sengupta explains it, and between the application of life imprisonment in Germany, as explained in Viewpoint 2-1, by Dirk van Zyl Smit? Do you think either India or Germany would provide a good blueprint for international standards on life imprisonment? Explain your answer.

2. Is it more humane to have a separate standard of sentencing for juveniles? Consider the way in which separate justice for juveniles functions in Singapore (Viewpoint 2-3) and the way in which juveniles are treated in adult prisons in Honduras (Viewpoint 2-4).

Chapter 3

1. Look again at the viewpoints by Jean-Marc Rouillan (3-2), Mustafa Akyol (3-3), and Merrill Goozner (3-6). Based on these viewpoints, discuss some ways in which inhumane treatment in prisons may be harmful for society as a whole.

2. The conditions faced by juvenile inmates in the United States, as discussed in Viewpoint 3-8, are less horrific than those faced by prisoners in Zimbabwe (Viewpoint 3-4) or in South Africa (Viewpoint 3-5). How bad do conditions in a prison have to be before they qualify as inhumane? (You may also want to refer to J.L. Murdoch's discussion in Viewpoint 3-1.)

Chapter 4

1. In Viewpoint 4-3, Andreas Lorenz notes that John Kamm has been able to obtain prisoner releases in China by compiling lists of prisoners. Do you think a similar tactic would work in releasing political prisoners in Iran or Cuba, based on the discussions by Golnaz Esfandiari and Dalia Acosta? Explain your reasoning.

2. Looking through all the viewpoints in this section, what do you think makes someone a political prisoner rather than a regular prisoner? Would the treatment of these prisoners (for example, of Falun Gong prisoners in Viewpoint 4-2) be acceptable if they were *not* political prisoners?

Organizations to Contact

The editors have compiled the following list of organizations concerned with the issues debated in this book. The descriptions are derived from materials provided by the organizations. All have publications or information available for interested readers. The list was compiled on the date of publication of the present volume; the information provided here may change. Be aware that many organizations take several weeks or longer to respond to inquiries, so allow as much time as possible.

American Civil Liberties Union (ACLU)
National Prison Project
1875 Connecticut Avenue NW, Suite 410
Washington, DC 20009
(202) 234-4830 • fax: (202) 234-4890
e-mail: aclu@aclu.org
Web site: www.aclu.org/prison/index.html

Formed in 1972, the American Civil Liberties Union's (ACLU's) National Prison Project serves as a national resource center and litigates cases to strengthen and protect adult and juvenile offenders' Eighth Amendment rights. It opposes electronic monitoring of offenders and the privatization of prisons. The project publishes the quarterly *National Prison Project Journal* and various booklets.

Amnesty International (AI)
5 Penn Plaza, New York, NY 10001
(212) 807-8400 • fax: (212) 627-1451
e-mail: admin-us@aiusa.org
Web site: www.amnesty.org

Made up of over 1.8 million members in over one hundred and fifty countries, Amnesty International (AI) is dedicated to promoting human rights worldwide. Since its inception in

1961, the organization has focused much of its effort on the eradication of torture. AI maintains an active news Web site, distributes numerous special reports on specific human rights issues including an annual report on the state of human rights in every country, and publishes the *Wire*, a monthly magazine.

European Committee for the Prevention of Torture and Inhuman or Degrading Treatment or Punishment (CPT)

Council of Europe, Strasbourg Cedex   F-67075
   France
+33 0388413939 • fax: +33 0388412772
e-mail: cptdoc@coe.int
Web site: www.cpt.coe.int

The European Committee for the Prevention of Torture and Inhuman or Degrading Treatment or Punishment (CPT) originated with the 1987 passage of the European Convention for the Prevention of Torture and Inhuman or Degrading Treatment or Punishment, an international treaty ratified by forty-five members of the European Council. The CPT performs site visits in participating countries to ensure that no torture or other inhuman treatment is taking place. It maintains a large online database detailing torture reports and site visits, and publishes numerous reports, standards, and reference documents pertaining to torture.

Families Against Mandatory Minimums (FAMM)

1612 K Street NW, Suite 700, Washington, DC   20006
(202) 822-6700 • fax: (202) 822-6704
e-mail: famm@famm.org
Web site: www.famm.org

Families Against Mandatory Minimums (FAMM) is an educational organization that works to repeal mandatory minimum sentences. It provides legislators, the public, and the media with information on and analyses of minimum-sentencing laws. FAMM publishes the quarterly newsletter *FAMMGram*.

HM Prison Service

Parliamentary, Correspondence and Briefing Unit
Cleland House, Page Street, London   SW1P 4LN
   United Kingdom
Web site: www.hmprisonservice.gov.uk

HM Prison Service is the government body responsible for prisons in the United Kingdom. It protects the public by providing humane prisons and rehabilitation services. HM Prison Service publishes *Prison Service Journal (PSJ)*. Select articles from this journal, press releases, reports, and other information are available on the HM Prison Service Web site.

Human Rights Watch (HRW)

350 Fifth Avenue, 34th Floor, New York, NY   10118-3299
(212) 290-4700 • fax: (212) 736-1300
e-mail: hrwnyc@hrw.org
Web site: www.hrw.org

In 1988, several large regional organizations dedicated to promoting human rights merged to form Human Rights Watch (HRW), a global watchdog group. HRW publishes numerous books, policy papers, and special reports including a comprehensive annual report, sponsors an annual film festival on human rights issues, and files lawsuits on behalf of those whose rights are violated.

John Howard Society of Canada (JHS)

809 Blackburn Mews, Kingston, ON
   K7P 2N6
   Canada
(613) 384-6272 • fax: (613) 384-1847
e-mail: national@johnhoward.ca
Web site: www.johnhoward.ca

The John Howard Society of Canada (JHS) advocates reform in the criminal justice system and monitors governmental policy to ensure fair and compassionate treatment of prisoners. It views imprisonment as a last resort. The organization provides education to the community, support services to at-risk youth, and rehabilitation programs to former inmates. Its Web site includes policy papers and briefs.

Just Detention International (JDI)
3325 Wilshire Boulevard, Suite 340, Los Angeles, CA   90010
(213) 384-1400 • fax: (213) 384-1411
e-mail: info@justdetention.org
Web site: www.justdetention.org

Just Detention International (JDI) is a human rights organiza-tion that seeks to end sexual abuse in all forms of detention. JDI is active in the United States and internationally in coun-tries such as South Africa, Mexico, and the Philippines. It works to hold governments accountable for sexual abuse, edu-cate the public, and provide resources for victims of prison sexual abuse. To further these goals, it conducts workshops and works with other human rights organizations. JDI pub-lishes news updates and reports on its Web site including *Im-proving Prison Oversight to Address Sexual Violence in Prisons.*

National Criminal Justice Reference Service (NCJRS)
U.S. Department of Justice, PO Box 6000
Rockville, MD   20849-6000
(301) 519-5500 • fax: (301) 519-5212
Web site: www.ncjrs.org

The National Criminal Justice Reference Service (NCJRS) is a federally funded resource offering justice and substance abuse information. It is one of the most extensive sources of infor-mation on criminal justice in the world. NCJRS provides topi-cal searches and reading lists on many areas of criminal justice including the death penalty. It publishes an annual report on capital punishment.

The Sentencing Project
514 Tenth Street NW, Suite 1000, Washington, DC   20004
(202) 628-0871 • fax: (202) 628-1091

e-mail: staff@sentencingproject.org
Web site: www.sentencingproject.org

The Sentencing Project provides public defenders and other public officials with information on establishing and improving alternative sentencing programs that provide convicted persons with positive and constructive options to incarceration. It promotes increased public understanding of the sentencing process and alternative sentencing programs. It publishes reports such as *No Exit: The Expanding Use of Life Sentences in America* and *Federal Crack Cocaine Sentencing*.

U.S. Department of Justice Federal Bureau of Prisons (BOP)
320 First Street NW, Washington, DC   20534
(202) 307-3198
e-mail: info@bop.gov
Web site: www.bop.gov

The U.S. Department of Justice Federal Bureau of Prisons (BOP) protects society by confining offenders in the controlled environments of prisons and community-based facilities. It believes in providing work and other self-improvement opportunities within these facilities to assist offenders in becoming law-abiding citizens. The bureau publishes the annual *State of the Bureau*.

Bibliography of Books

Ervand Abrahamian — *Tortured Confessions: Prison and Public Recantations in Modern Iran.* Berkeley, CA: University of California Press, 1999.

Pat Carlen, ed. — *Women and Punishment: The Struggle for Justice.* Devon, UK: Willan Publishing, 2002.

Pat Carlen and Anne Worrall — *Analysing Women's Imprisonment.* Devon, UK: Willan Publishing, 2004.

Michael Cavadino and James Dignan — *The Penal System: An Introduction.* 4th ed. London, UK: SAGE Publications Ltd., 2007.

Elaine Crawley — *Doing Prison Work: The Public and Private Lives of Prison Officers.* Devon, UK: Willan Publishing, 2004.

Chris Cunneen and Rob White — *Juvenile Justice: Youth and Crime in Australia.* 3rd ed. New York: Oxford University Press, 2007.

Laura B. Edge — *Locked Up: A History of the U.S. Prison System.* Minneapolis, MN: Twenty-First Century Books, 2009.

Michael Harris — *Con Game: The Truth About Canada's Prisons.* Toronto, Ontario: McClelland & Stewart, Ltd., 2003.

Mike Hough, Rob Allen, and Enver Solomon, eds. — *Tackling Prison Overcrowding: Build More Prisons? Sentence Fewer Offenders?* Bristol, UK: The Policy Press, 2008.

Yvonne Jewkes and Helen Johnston, eds. *Prison Readings: A Critical Introduction to Prisons and Imprisonment.* Devon, UK: Willan Publishing, 2006.

Jean Kellaway *The History of Torture & Execution: From Early Civilization Through Medieval Times to the Present.* London, UK: Mercury Books, 2003.

Soon Ok Lee *Eyes of the Tailless Animals: Prison Memoirs of a North Korean Woman.* Bartlesville, OK: Living Sacrifice Book Company, 1999.

David Matas and David Kilgour *Bloody Harvest: Organ Harvesting of Falun Gong Practitioners in China.* Woodstock, Ontario: Seraphim Editions, 2009.

Norval Morris and David J. Rothman, eds. *The Oxford History of the Prison: The Practice of Punishment in Western Society.* New York: Oxford University Press, 1995.

John Muncie *Youth and Crime.* London, UK: SAGE Publications Ltd., 2004.

Ahmed Othmani *Beyond Prison: The Fight to Reform Prison Systems Around the World.* New York: Berghahn Books, 2008.

Christian Parenti *Lockdown America: Police and Prisons in the Age of Crisis.* New York: Verso Press, 2000.

Mitchel P. Roth *Prison and Prison Systems: A Global Encyclopedia.* Westport, CT: Greenwood Press, 2006.

Jeremy Sarkin   *Human Rights in African Prisons.*
Athens, OH: Ohio University Press,
2008.

Elizabeth S. Scott *Rethinking Juvenile Justice.* Cam-
and Laurence   bridge, MA: Harvard University
Steinberg   Press, 2008.

Rita J. Simon   *The Crimes Women Commit: The*
and Heather   *Punishments They Receive.* 3rd ed.
Ahn-Redding   Lanham, MD: Lexington Books,
2005.

Dirk van Zyl Smit *Principles of European Prison Law and*
and Sonja   *Policy: Penology and Human Rights.*
Snacken   New York: Oxford University Press,
2009.

Roger Smith   *Political Prisoners.* Broomall, PA: Ma-
son Crest Publishers, 2006.

World Health   *Health in Prisons: A WHO Guide to*
Organization   *the Essentials in Prison Health.*
Copenhagen, Denmark: World Health
Organization, 2007.

Index

Geographic headings and page numbers in **boldface** refer to viewpoints about that country or region.